VENTURA STARWAY

MISSION 6

BLACK OCEAN: MIRTH & MAYHEM

J.S. MORIN

Magical Scrivener Press
www.magicalscrivener.com

Publisher's Note: This is a work of fiction. Names, characters, places, and incidents are a product of the author's imagination. Locales and public names are sometimes used for atmospheric purposes. Any resemblance to actual people, living or dead, or to businesses, companies, events, institutions, or locales is completely coincidental.

Ordering Information: Special discounts are available on quantity purchases by corporations, associations, and others. For details, contact the publisher at the address above.

J.S. Morin — First Edition

ISBN: 978-1-64355-615-4

Printed in the United States of America

VENTURA STARWAY
MISSION 6

THE CRACK of a pop-top perked up Chuck Ramsey's ears as he sat with his feet up on the dashboard of the *Radio City*. He'd been staring out into the depths of the galaxy with a front-row view of a number-for-a-name gas giant with rings that the kids had dubbed Ballerina due to the "tutu" it wore. The spectacular sight had put Becky in the mood, and he was enjoying his afterglow while she showered.

Clad in just a bathrobe, he ventured back to see whether his wife had gone straight from shower to fridge or whether Mort was up late.

As he made his way barefoot, Chuck swayed hips and elbows to some Bad Company that had gotten stuck in his head. He didn't care that he probably looked ridiculous; he knew he was no dancer. He'd been in-character enough planetside that he needed to let loose a little, let the facade sit in its charging dock, ready to go next time he needed it.

"Couldn't sleep?" Mort asked from the couch when Chuck arrived.

"Some nights, she won't let me," he replied with a sly grin.

Mort grunted. "If you can keep that robe closed, you're welcome to join me." The wizard patted the adjacent cushion.

Snickering, Chuck made his way to the fridge. "I'd take pointers. I gotta think a wizard must know all sorts of tricks when it comes to wearing a robe."

"Undergarments are key," Mort replied deadpan. "Unless he's the guest of honor at a particular sort of party, you take a wizard out of his robes, and he'd still be legally allowed into most offices and any restaurant without a dress code. Think of it more like a shin-length suit coat."

"Huh... who'd have thought. I'd always thought of a robe as more of a tall kilt with sleeves."

"Don't let a Scotsman hear that," Mort warned teasingly. "I once made a flippant comment about kilt-wearing and lost an evening getting educated about clan tartan patterns."

Chuck shook his head as he took the handle of the fridge in hand. "You and I have led very different—shit."

"Indeed. I was just thinking to myself: I don't shit anything like a technologist. I—"

"No. We're down to our last cold beer. Might have to save this one for the Beckster and grab a warm one from the cargo hold."

Mort cleared his throat. "Or... maybe she'll opt not to drink before bed."

"Nah. Not revved up like I got her. Her bedside stash is out. She asked me to stock it for her this afternoon, but..." Chuck shrugged. "I got busy."

"I mean, we've been straight out these last weeks," Mort replied. "Dropping into astral, out of astral, back in... I daresay we've seen half the sights in the galaxy by now. Pace of... what... one every two or three days? Phew..."

The wizard could be damnably subtle at times. He must have thought Chuck was sleepy or something to wield his verbal mallet with such open verve. Choosing not to march into a war of words with a one-man army, Chuck instead headed back to the cargo hold to see what warm brew he'd be swilling until its next of kin cooled off in the fridge.

Crates upon crates stacked akimbo, shoulder high and balanced with amateur optimism. The disorganization was half laziness, half lazy-as-a-foxness. Customs inspectors were human—most of them, anyway. They were on schedules, evaluated on throughput, responsible for delays. Keeping things tidy would get them in and out quicker. Importantly, it would also make it shitloads easier to find stuff.

Chuck liked the option of playing a shell game as he shifted supplies around, hiding certain minor contraband he didn't want either confiscated or taxed, depending on the contents.

Today, however, his own cargo hold was conspiring to hide his beer.

"Ow! Dammit!" he cursed as he stubbed a bare toe shifting a box of diapers that Rhiannon had outgrown needing. "Why do we even keep these things?"

The aftermarket for half a crate of Cuddlies sized for a 16 kg toddler flashed through Chuck's mind briefly before a shake of his head chased the thoughts away.

"She can use the toilet," Becky commented from the doorway. "But there's always the chance of a next one."

The voice from an unnoticed observer startled Chuck, who banged a knee as he turned to see his wife in nothing but a pair of towels. She watched him with crossed arms and the last cold beer clutched in one hand.

"I hate to admit this... but I think I let us run out of beer," Chuck said as he gathered himself.

"We didn't exactly shop for a long trip before bugging off Vega. We'll swing over and make a beer run tomorrow."

Chuck snorted. As if it were that simple. "It's not like we're on the Earth-Luna express lane. Can't just order ahead and hit a fly-thru. And looking for beer, I noticed we're getting low on cereal, toothsoap, and pretty much every kind of cartridge for the food processor."

"So, like, a real supply run, then?" She took a chug of beer.

Nodding thoughtfully, Chuck pondered where he could find all that stuff at rock-bottom prices. When nothing came to mind, he realized he needed a location that doubled as a money-making opportunity. Gigs had dried up since Vega IX, and income was growing on the list of dire family issues.

Chuck snapped his fingers. "I got it."

"Got what?" Becky asked as he whisked by, grabbing her beer and taking a deep swallow before handing it back.

"Hang tight, babe. Don't wanna get your hopes up."

Chuck spent the next two hours making comms, staying up past the chrono rolling over into tomorrow. It wasn't common knowledge. You had to know someone who knew someone, and old info was as good as none at all. In the vast emptiness of the Black Ocean, out of range of every sensor array in ARGO and beyond, finding it by chance was like picking a particular speck of dust out of Saturn's ring. Finally, it was Lou Williams who provided the info Chuck was looking for.

"*Yeah, I'm inbound now myself. Transmitting coordinates for Ventura Convoy.*"

Mort squinted out the window against the glare of a star looming all too close. The sting in his eyes was worth the pain. Far from empty, this planetless system bore witness to a sight Mort could hardly believe.

"Egad, it's like the Bermuda Triangle's dung cellar. How many ships can get lost at once?"

The answer defied quick counting. Hundreds, anyway. One big one, a corpse among a swarm of flies. Sizes were impossible to judge, but there was a lower limit to how small a ship could get and still have a living person cooped up inside. That made the big one enormous at the least, mind-boggling at the most.

And Mort's mind didn't boggle easily.

"It's a piece of crap," Brad commented quietly. "Rickety old supertransport they wouldn't let into Sol because the insurance peeps would croak."

Behind them, Chuck had overheard. "It's not the *Convoy Queen*. It's the gestalt. Take it all in." He breathed deep and swept spread arms together and upward. "Every ship out there is part of the convoy. Every last one. Soon, we'll be one of them."

At a glance, Mort identified an issue that he hoped wasn't lost on the two male Ramseys. "Shouldn't one of you boys be flying?"

Chuck waved off the notion. "Becky might not fly, but she can mind the controls while we get a flight vector. I can take over when we get a docking clearance."

Brad cocked his head and avoided eye contact with his father.

"Fine," Chuck barked, not missing the pantomime. "You can dock us. There's no planetary laws. No orbit; no orbital control—"

"Nothing to do."

"Hey, you wanna dock or not?" Chuck demanded.

"Do I get a vote?" Mort asked.

"No," Chuck and Brad shouted in unison. Never had they sounded more alike since Mort had known them.

"Look, it's not like I need the practice. I just don't like the way *you* dock," Brad replied. "This whole convoy is a terra trap. We could restock on plenty of low-sec planets or space stations. Places that don't trust newsfeeds or cross-reference new arrivals against ships that left Vega IX around November 3rd. Why can't we go to any of those?"

Chuck smirked. "You just can't live without an omni connection."

"You won't pay for the piggyback signal from the queen ship."

They'd lost Mort. This conversation had boiled down to the vagaries of the convoy's technological failings. Rather than allow himself to get tangled up in a futile effort to comprehend the iniquities at issue and risk his mind snapping like an overstretched hair elastic, Mort settled back in at the window, marveling at the epic scope of humanity's stupidity.

Hundreds upon hundreds of ships, each stranded a trillion miles from civilization with a few puffs of captive air and an overcomplicated gizmo to ferry them around. Thousands of lives dangling from a spider's web.

Some part of Mort's brain was listening as Chuck and Brad argued. It was like watching a pair of fencers who were afraid of getting hit. Probing thrusts. Nothing intended to risk a counterattack.

"I don't suppose a ship that big could take a little magic..."

The argument stopped in its tracks.

"Whoa. No magicko, compadre. We might be going a quadrillion kilometers an hour—"

"We aren't," Brad clarified *sotto voce*.

"But that's not any special feat when you haven't stopped at a shipyard in decades. The *Convoy Queen* operates on a shoestring budget, basically just a co-op to share common costs and keep the life support running. In fact, there's a pretty strict no-magic policy. Never really stopped to consider before..."

Unsurprising. Chuck's inability to plan ahead accounted for the majority of his life's troubles. Not that Mort considered himself a shining exemplar of life outcomes. He'd resume tossing stones once he turned the glass of his house back to glassteel.

Mort heaved a sigh. "Suppose I can hold out as long as it takes."

Chuck clapped him on the shoulder. "I'll make it up to you. Next stop can be your pick."

A twitch of his lip was all the smile Mort could muster. He knew there would be a lull when Azrael stopped indirectly sponsoring Chuck's comedy career. But the alternative hadn't, as Mort suspected, been extended stays on planets like Carson.

"I'll give it some thought."

Mort didn't know where he'd take the *Radio City* if Chuck kept his promise. But he knew it would be someplace where he could do all the magic he liked and didn't have to trip over finicky doodads.

If such a place existed in this modern galaxy.

The *Radio City* slid into the docking station with a reassuring *thunk*. Chuck breathed a sigh of relief. Somehow, no matter how many times the kid did it, he always suspected Brad would fumble the controls at the last second and kill them all. How could the kid be such a fuckup at 99 percent of all human endeavors yet pilot a starship like a seasoned pro?

As if sensing his old man's skepticism, Brad leaned back, laced his fingers, and stretched elaborately. "Chillax. I got this boat on rails."

Before Chuck came back with a pin to pop that inflated ego the boy was growing, the ship jolted. A metallic *clang* like an off-key gong set his teeth on edge. Despite the engines being powered down and the vessel docked, it was tempting to still ride Brad's ass for it.

"Magnetic docking clamp engaged. Current rate is 50T per hour for each full or partial hour. Enjoy your stay aboard the Convoy Queen."

If the sound of the clamp had rattled Chuck's nerves, the whorehouse model of docking fee grated on his bank account. 100T a night was core-world pricing. Even on Earth, public lots couldn't get away with charging over 200T. The split share for upkeep on a place like Carson came to a little over ten, and that came with free use of the hibachis and campground.

Chuck dropped a heavy hand on his son's shoulder. "You can run aboard and have a quick look, but get us back into the convoy before the hour's up. Keep your datapad handy. I'll comm for pickup."

"Aw, come on. I want to shop."

"With what money?" Chuck inquired. It wouldn't be the first time the kid had squirreled away a nest egg without him noticing. Coming out of Vega IX, he'd have been more surprised if Brad hadn't scammed himself a little something from the well-to-do locals.

"Fine. Window shopping."

Chuck snorted. "Look. Go ahead. Enjoy the amenities. When you get bored, hustle back. But anything that costs me another hour of that extortion comes out of *your* pocket, even if you end up in debt, got it?"

A wicked grin spread on the boy's face. "I can run a Loan 'em and Leave 'em on a convoy shark?"

"No." Chuck let a deadly serious settle into his voice. "No loans. Especially not blasterpoint loans."

Brad deflated. "I could pull it off, ya know. I'm underage. My criminal record is clean."

"For now..."

"And I've got a completely forgettable face."

"Except for digital cameras."

"Mort's been teaching me how not to let cameras see me."

"How's that been going?"

"He says I'd have more luck wearing a mask."

"Look. Your yapping is costing terras. You've probably got some friends out in the convoy. Just don't dock with anyone we don't know."

Brad perked up. "You know something. Who's riding Ventura with us?"

"Uncle Lou." Chuck shrugged. "Who knows who else. Knock yourself out scoping the lanes."

"Anji?" Lou was Anji Williams's *actual* uncle. Brad knew which family trees among the nomads were planted side by side and which were grafted.

"Galak's corewards, last I heard. You can bark up that tree some other time."

Brad screwed up his face in a scowl. "Fine. Maybe I can snag some snacks from the core before my exile." He got up from the pilot's chair and headed for the airlock.

By the time Chuck got there, Brad was gone. Becky awaited him, fussing with the littles' outfits and double-checking her day bag. Looking down at the pair, it occurred to him that the littles weren't quite so little anymore. Rhi could speak in sentences and type her full name, and Mikey was getting to the point where he had hobbies and opinions. Rhi was a load of rocks, and Mikey was just flat out too heavy to carry around. Both wore their hair in pigtails—braiding hair was one of Mikey's new hobbies.

Damn. Chuck considered that he might need to get started on another baby. Losing them out the far end of the nest wasn't nearly the same blow to his ego as seeing the youngest ones growing up.

"OK, now you two are going to stick close. Mommy's going

shopping, and if you're both good, you can each get something. Now, if you get lost, what do you do?"

Mikey recited, "Ask to comm the *Radio City*."

Becky stared down Rhi until the little girl answered, "I live on *Radio City*."

Chuck tousled two heads on his way by. "Great job. Now just don't go running off on your mom. Brad'll be back in a few hours to pick us up. Enjoy the bazaar. Hey, anyone seen Mort?"

"Here," Mort replied with leaden enthusiasm. "Don't mind me. I'll take my stroll in arcane purgatory. At least I won't die of the tedium with unstretched legs."

"That's the spirit."

Wife, kids, and wizard departed. Chuck hung back to close and passcode the ship. If the boy forgot the combination, he could damn well fork over the docking fee as punishment. There were places in the galaxy where that kind of forgetfulness could be deadly. Chuck was willing to smack Brad upside the piggy bank to teach him that lesson.

By the time Chuck reached the transit concourse, Mort was long gone. Becky lagged at the edge of the conveyor as a merchant with a long load of crates, assistants, and loose wares rumbled past.

"Daddy's coming with us," Mikey exclaimed.

Peace and quiet would be in short supply during the visit to the city-sized swap meet. Chuck had at least counted on a different sort of unceasing din. "Well, for the walkway ride at least."

The merchant's inventory cleared out and rolled on ahead, leaving room for four Ramseys to hop aboard. The belt moved at a brisk walking pace, faster than either of the littles could have sustained—probably Becky, too. Chuck, with his long legs, liked to think he was merely riding in style, saving his wind for the talking he'd be doing once they arrived.

"Don't go buying high," Becky warned in a low voice. "We gotta steady our flow until the digits start rolling again."

"Don't go *getting* high," Chuck shot back, trying to avoid drawing interest from the two children whose attention fixated on the wonders of the grand cargo hold that opened up over them. "That's our major expense right after fuel and before food."

"Ain't."

Chuck wasn't going to have this argument here and now. "I'll buy what we need, and I'll get it at the price I can get. When Brad comes back for us, I'll probably have barter deals in place for half the junk in the hold that we're not using."

"Like those nappies?"

"And the golf clubs, that flavor of Frooti Juice no one will drink, the baby toys, teething rings, that busted-ass guitar that won't stay in tune... hell, if I can get a deal to marry Brad off to some tesud colonial princess, I'm making that deal. Kid'd play ball until the money changed hands."

"No scams."

Chuck lowered his voice even farther. "No. Not on your life. This is where we come up ahead. Core worlds have been ripping us off lately." He caught her 'no shit' look. "I mean worse than usual. And the colonies aren't easy pickings these days."

"Folks here expect it."

"Right on. Their own fault. We're part of the natural order."

Becky glanced down at the kiddos. "Just you be careful. Ya catch my drift?"

Chuck leaned close and whispered, "Just you wait, Sunshine. I score big, maybe we celebrate in a way that keeps those baby toys and teething rings around a while longer." He gave her ass a quick squeeze.

They kissed before parting, with Becky remaining on the rumbling strip of moving floor as Chuck hopped lightly to solid ground.

The main hold of the *Convoy Queen* rose six stories high, crisscrossed by catwalks where armed guards kept the peace. Below, row upon row upon row of rental retail space sprawled out in a grid. Spacers, nomads, grifters, merchants, traders, thieves, brokers, collectors, and opportunists hawked their wares and dealt their deals. There was no telling what one might find for sale.

From name-brand cereals to knockoff pharmaceuticals and everything in between, finding it on the *Convoy Queen* was just a matter of time, patience, and haggling.

Chuck *loved* the haggling.

━━━

Brad breathed deep, savoring the odd palette of scents ranging from discount cologne to exotic meats. This was commerce at its best. No shopping plaza or planetside store could compete with the raw, unfettered capitalism of the great swap meet aboard the *Convoy Queen*. More than half the vessels in Ventura Convoy were operating on skeleton crews while their people bought, sold, and bartered whatever goods they had or needed.

The perfect environment for a shark to eat his fill among the fish.

It was also too damn hot to be wearing extra layers.

Brad had considered running back to the ship to ditch his jacket, but he'd also counted on it as part of his personal security. The sitharn security force patrolling the catwalks overhead might have preferred the heat, but Brad would have taken his chances looking out for his own safety and letting the life support blow a little cool air into the swap meet. It wasn't like the lizards were even keen-eyed enough to spot pickpockets, let alone care.

In his left jacket pocket, Brad kept a hold on his large-denomination hardcoin. In his right, he clutched two golf-ball-sized objects, twirling them one around the other as they scraped together and rubbed hard edges across his palm. The constant reminder kept him focused even if it wasn't comfortable.

Still, it was necessary. If he let his eyes wander and the wonderment set in, he might lose hours or even whole days in aimless wandering, sampling far-flung foods and purchasing a cadre of knickknacks he had no use for.

Hawkers extolled the virtues of every errant path Brad might take.

A guy in a phony tuxedo hailed him from behind a table laden with data crystals. "Hey, kid. No omni got ya down? I got every game's come out the past ten years. I can—"

"No thanks, old man. Here's a tip, no kid wants to be called 'hey, kid.' You lost a sale before I knew what you were selling." He didn't stop to let the guy argue.

A sizzling wok wafted something beefy-smelling. The cook in a plastipaper hat waved a spatula. "Try some of my—"

"Already ate," Brad countered without breaking stride.

The shadiest guy Brad ever laid eyes on—and that was saying something—wore a shabby gray trench coat and faded brown fedora along with shader lenses indoors. He operated out of a suitcase opened on a folding table, facing him so that passersby couldn't see its contents. "Hey, pal. I got what you need right here." His voice was gravelly and modulated to be just loud enough to be heard and no louder.

Curiosity got the better of Brad. He stopped and slouched skeptically. "All right. I'll bite. What is it I need?"

Mr. Shady palmed something and used the flap of his trench coat to shield his big reveal from foot traffic. Brad was just glad he was clothed underneath the coat. What he showed was a silver capsule with a tiny plunger on one side.

Brad shrugged. "I'm not looking for a high."

"Not for you," Mr. Shady clarified. "For her."

"Her?" Brad asked, hoping he wasn't following but dreading that he might be.

"It's new. Aphrodite. Hit her with this when you've got her alone, and she'll be all over you for hours. I can give you a discount on the first one but—"

Brad put up a hand, momentarily leaving his hardcoin unattended in his pocket. "Gonna stop ya right there. There's a moment in a guy's life when he realizes that he's incapable of attracting the opposite sex. I suppose you got there and decided to go all slaver chem about it."

The shady drug peddler gritted his teeth. "Shut up, kid. You don't want any, just move along."

"Naw," Brad replied. "I gotta help a guy in your situation. See? Me, I figured out it's easier finding girls who want some and applying for the job rather than picking one I want and convincing them they want me, too. You don't need pills; you need a personality transplant. Polish that resume, not your knob."

"Hey!" The dealer flinched toward Brad but didn't throw the punch he threatened.

Grinning, Brad dodged backward. "I see that's a non-starter. Maybe I can help you advertise, at least."

Brad scanned the pedestrian traffic squeezing past in both directions. It didn't take him long to find a likely candidate. "Hey, big sister," he called out.

It was old slang, but the woman in the ballistic vest with colonial militia patches on her sleeve perked up. She also had an empty holster worn at her thigh, which meant she was so accustomed to wearing it that even when she had to leave her weapon before coming aboard, she kept it on. "What, kid? I'm kinda in the middle of—"

"It's important," Brad assured her.

"Shut *up!*" the drug dealer snarled urgently.

"Fine," the colonial veteran said. "What's the scam?"

Brad hooked a thumb. "This guy's peddling sex slave chem to any old shitter with terras. I was hoping you might know someone who'd be interested."

"Why the *fuck* would I...?" Then, it seemed to dawn on her what Brad was implying. What he was *truly* implying. She looked the trench-coated miscreant up and down. Despite the fact he was probably five centimeters taller, she made him look tiny. "Yeah. You know what? I think I know some people who'd buy wholesale."

"You... you do?"

The colonial soldier smiled slowly. "Uh-huh. How about you give me the name of your ship, and we can dock for some real commerce. None of this small-scale stuff."

With an exchange of winks, Brad left the drug slaver in the capable hands of some retired gunnery sergeant, if his understanding of common military insignia was correct.

While stirring up a little good trouble was fun, the *Radio City* was docked and costing him terras the longer he left it unattended.

And he still had an important task left.

It took the better part of two hours. He swore Robert Ventura had cooked up the scheme of leaving the swap meet unlabeled and uncategorized just to drive up docking times. But eventually, through a combination of word of mouth and footsore plodding, Brad came across a jeweler.

"You a buyer, seller, or both?" Brad asked, trying to keep

the guy from pegging Brad before he had a chance to explain his situation. The jeweler was busy, eyes glued to a tabletop scanner. As he waited, Brad made a show of examining the wares in the glassteel case on wheels that doubled as the man's storefront counter.

It was mostly the type of jewelry that rotten husbands and boyfriends purchased to douse the fires their own misdeeds had set. They were desperate greeting cards with implied messages ranging from "I forgot it was your birthday until the last minute"—a simple silver bracelet—to a necklace in the form of a diamond river that could have convincingly argued, "I swear I didn't know that having two other families on separate colonies was something you'd mind."

When the jeweler looked up, he raised one eyebrow behind his microscope goggles. The lenses probably did something to help with appraising gemstones, so Brad didn't complain, but they made the guy's eyes look freakishly huge. "Can I help you?"

"Looking for an estimate. Maybe a sale."

Brad, a victim of more eye-rolls than he could count, knew damn well when someone meant one without actually following through on it. With a sigh born out of sheer professionalism, the jeweler asked, "What do you have?"

Extracting his right hand from his pocket, Brad folded it open to display two purple gems.

"Where did you get them?" The question didn't sound accusing, but considering how evasive the guy's whole demeanor was, Brad chose to answer obliquely.

"Payment for services rendered. Didn't ask for certificates or that sort of shit."

For once, the truth served him well. Mort hadn't said where he'd gotten two enormous rocks that would have looked gaudy in a king's crown. Despite the question eating him up inside,

Brad knew he was better off not knowing. What answer would have been safe to hear when a skyscraper flattens itself around a guy who walks away without a scratch? The previous owner was almost certainly dead. Brad didn't need the details.

The jeweler took one of the stones and held it up. His lenses whirred, and the outer frame twisted. His eyes went six kinds of wonky before he finally declared, "Well, I'll be."

"You'll be buying them off me for...?" Brad trailed off, leaving a convenient blank for the jewelry expert to fill in.

"Twelve hundred hard."

"Each?" Brad queried hopefully. "And I'd like to be paid digital."

"For the pair, assuming the second amethyst checks out. And I don't give Ventura a cut of my profits to use his connection."

It was the only omni connection around. Anyone who wanted access could get it, Brad knew from Dad's tirades, but only at a steep price.

"I'll cover it out of my payout," Brad insisted. "But only for the full price of 2400."

"I won't give Ventura the business. He lives like a king off the terras he siphons from our veins. I barely make a profit on these trips as it is."

As negotiating ploys went, it sounded weak. As a principled stand against a commercial paradigm, Brad didn't know where to go with his next argument. He sure as fuck didn't want to bring more hardcoin back to the *Radio City*. It was a struggle keeping his current stash hidden.

Maybe he could find an exchange broker willing to take yet another cut of the pie to ship his terras into core world banks in digital form.

But he sure wasn't going to do it for a measly twelve hundred.

"Thanks, but no thanks, pal. I know what these are worth. You're taking me for a ride even at my price. Fuck yours."

"Come crawling back, and it's a thousand for the both," the jeweler called after him.

Brad wasn't worried. There were a million shops on this barge. Even at 50T an hour, he could come out ahead shopping for a smoking-hot deal.

———

The air was regurgitated, fed back to the vessel's inhabitants like a mama bird did with her chicks.

The landscape was an imitation of the open-air bazaars of pre-spaceflight Earth.

Every food on offer mimicked a dish common in colonies across ARGO space.

Mort doubted that even the people were real; heck, *he* was incognito.

The nomad wizard had no overarching goal in visiting the swap meet. He wasn't on secondhand Convocation business, wasn't looking for dark wizards, wasn't even looking to shop, for that matter.

Long strides put him at odds with the slow-moving sludge of gawkers and eyeball shoppers clogging the thoroughfares. Mort was thin enough to weave through most of the knotted snarls, secretly amused that he could have a path wider than the span of his arms in an instant if he clued these commerce-crazed yahoos to his true identity.

Idle curiosity kept Mort's eyes flitting back and forth in his skull, taking in the sights, such as they were. The sheer variety for sale impressed him. Given a lifetime, he wouldn't have come up with a full list so diverse.

Kitchen gadgets of every description.

Clothes for all genders, occasions, sizes, and even species. If Mort ever needed a shark costume for a juvenile tesud to wear for Halloween, the Ventura Convoy had him covered.

Personal care products promised to treat conditions and groom Mort in ways he'd never considered.

There were board games and jigsaw puzzles, yarn for knitting, thread for sewing, and kiddie clay for molding young minds.

Food came in pre-scienced crates, raw in both produce and meat forms, or served hot and fresh by chefs of dubious qualification.

Larger stalls offered furniture, ship parts, or small vehicles.

Unlicensed pharmacists peddled drugs that Mort presumed to span the gamut from mainstream to highly illicit, yet for the life of him, he could only guess between the two. But for all he knew, there were black-market wart creams and prescription hallucinogens floating around the storefronts.

Oh, and of course, there was smut everywhere.

It continually boggled Mort's sensibilities that most technophiles seemed unable to either quell their animal urges or find someone to pair off with for long-term mutual satisfaction. Outliers... those he understood. But the pervasiveness of the carnal goods and services industry seemed so utterly wasteful.

Some hours into his roaming, Mort stumbled upon the first peddler who captured his attention and stopped his feet.

"You there, you have the look of a man who might enjoy owning a piece of the arcane," a man in a floppy-pointed purple hat called out to him.

Stepping out of the stubbornly torpid traffic flow, Mort entered a square three paces across, lined with shelves bearing oddities ranging from mineralogical to bijouterie. Ignoring the salesman for the moment, Mort scanned the wares with his hands tucked away in the front pocket of his sweatshirt.

"Be ye a gentleman of acquisitional countenance or of a less sophisticated and purely appreciative manner?"

Rather than pick at the man's diction or cringeworthy attempt at Arthurian vocabulary, Mort decided to inquire about the objects for sale. "What's this one do?" He pointed with his nose toward a twig with a faceted piece of red glass jammed into the tip in imitation of a ruby.

The pointy-hatted huckster cleared his throat. "Well, that one is the Wand of Amun Ra. It was once owned by—"

"I asked what it did, not who owned it. Do you know or not?"

Hanging around Chuck had honed Mort's ear for bullshit. It had also oversharpened his blade to the point of brittleness.

"Well, you see, no one can be entirely sure, since the secret to—"

"And how much you charging for it?"

A pleasant grin dimpled the saleswizard's cheeks. "Well, for an astute collector such as yourself, I could let it go for as little as thirty-five hundred."

"It's a twig and a bit of glass."

"Whatever its origins may be, by dint of arcane exposure, it has transcended to become so much more."

For reasons Mort would have to examine in quieter hours, this charlatan was getting beneath his skin. Mort stepped to the next shelf and hefted a sea-smoothed stone painted with the Aramaic words for "wind foot." "And what, pray tell, is this one?"

"I wouldn't handle that one without gloves. That's—"

Whatever explanation was forthcoming shifted course as Mort scratched away the paint with a fingernail.

"Hey! Stop that! You're defiling a priceless antique. That stone is thousands of years old!"

"Stone's older than that," Mort corrected pedantically. "More like millions. But the paint reeks of science. Tell me, is there a damn bit of magic in this whole store?" He set down the rock and tucked his hands back in his front pocket.

"Sir, I'm going to have to ask you to move along. I must devote my attention to *paying* customers."

There wasn't another customer anywhere to be seen. Unless the man had a following among ratatoret, there was no place in the cramped booth for a customer to hide. As far as passersby, many glanced over, but few so much as slowed on their way past.

Mort stepped closer and lowered his voice. The pervasive din of hundreds of other conversations provided cover from nosy ears. "Look here, you disreputable cretin. I know a thing or three about magic. And I know there are laws against peddling phony artifacts."

"We're well outside Convocation jurisdiction, and magic is forbidden on the *Convoy Queen*. In fact, customers aren't even allowed to test my wares for fear of—"

"Of getting found out to be fakes and forgeries," Mort finished for him. "You operate here because you let the fellows in charge know they're junk. So, they don't care. Well, the fellows I work for care. And they keep a row of heads in jars— still alive and begging for death—of insolent technologists who besmirch the reputation of the Convocation."

The huckster's nostrils flared as he verged on hyperventilation. "Give me an hour. I'll be gone. You'll never see hide nor hair of me again."

"Eh?" Mort scoffed. "What gave you the impression I wanted you gone? I'm willing to ignore this whole encounter for the right price."

"How much?"

Ahh, here was the haggling with which Chuck seemed so enamored. If he couldn't be a wizard on the *Convoy Queen*, he could at least get his kicks being an outlaw.

"How much you got?"

Chuck shook hands with a rough-looking spacer wearing an overcoat and knit cap despite the heat aboard the *Convoy Queen*. The guy had a hydraulic grip and skin like burlap. But he was also a reliable home goods trader who'd come highly recommended by names Chuck trusted—well, as much as Chuck trusted anyone's word.

"Thanks, Pete. I really thought I'd have to make a lot more stops than this."

Pete Mazmer nodded behind a bushy beard that might have contained a smile if someone gave it a trim. "Give my folk some time to crate it up, then rendezvous with the *Mazmer Piano*. We'll contact you when it's ready for pickup. What kind of docking you got?"

"Standard civilian astrogation Type 4."

"No worries, then. Catch you soon." Pete waved as Chuck took his leave.

Reviewing his purchases, Chuck tapped checkboxes on his datapad. Even without an omni link, he could use it as a shopping list.

Toothsoap.

Oat Zeroes.

Pastrami cartridges.

Cheddar cartridges.

Rye cartridges… all sized for a class-4

food processor without the diagonal cutting
option.

That did it. Chuck's list went all green. With a smile, he
headed for the washroom line, no longer afraid he'd be losing
valuable negotiating time as he stood for up to an hour waiting
to piss.

He took his place at the cordoned zone of spacers waiting
their turn for the facilities. More convoy patrons filed in and
took places behind him. One of the underrated gems of the
Convoy Queen was free, clean, comfortable washrooms. It was
about the only service on board that *was* free, and Chuck
cynically suspected it was just to avoid the messes of guys
trying to hold out and failing.

The line was a trap, too, a captive audience for hucksters
with absolutely no shame.

"Get your prophyls here!" one shouted. "Enjoy the firing
range knowing all you're packing is blanks!"

"Keep hydrated," another bellowed, pushing a cart with a
wobbly repulsor and waving bottled water for all to see. "It
takes three weeks to starve, but you can die of thirst in days."

Chuck's favorite peddler—for sheer gall and ingenuity—
toted a backpack laden with boxes and hoisted one high to draw
attention. "Skip the line. Vaporizing catheters. Safe,
comfortable, compatible with all major life support filters.
Patented smell suppression keeps your ship fresh as your
bladder enjoys a vacation."

With top-of-the-lungs commerce surrounding him on all
sides, it took a moment for Chuck to realize one of the voices
was calling his name.

"Chuck? CHUCK? Chuck! There you are!"

Tall as he was, it took standing on tiptoe for Chuck to spot
the speaker. He'd never have accused Lou Williams of

possessing a voice that stood out in a crowd, but that face he'd know anywhere.

"Lou! You old rascal. How ya doin'?"

Lou wove through the parade of vendors and came up alongside Chuck.

"Hey, no cuttin' tha line!" the guy behind them protested.

"He's here on business, not pissness," Chuck retorted. Ignoring the sourpuss, Chuck embraced his buddy. "Thought I'd have to go ship-to-ship and find you here."

"No man's got a bladder of stone," Lou replied with a grin permanently fixed in place. "But if you can dam it up a little while longer, I'd got something you wanna hear."

"Can it wait ten minutes?" Chuck asked. Then, reconsidering his math, he sized up the line ahead of him. "Or maybe fifty?"

"Ditch the urinal stampede. I'm docked."

Chuck didn't need to be told twice. If Lou had the *Rex Piscis* hooked up to the *Convoy Queen*, he was on the clock, leaking terras from a punctured bank account. "Lead on."

Along the way, the pair chatted, catching up for the year and change since they'd crossed paths on Carson. There had been some hard feelings in the wake of the *Radio City's* sudden departure, but the disappearance of a sheriff's deputy and his brother-in-law had hinted at enough extenuating circumstances that the other nomads had blown orbit in short order. After all, no one wanted to stick around and answer questions when they might get arrested for wrong answers.

Once the airlock door sealed behind Chuck, Lou breathed a sigh of relief. "Safe."

Chuck snickered. "I know it's a little rough around the edges, but Ventura Convoy's as safe as you get around here."

"'Around here' is literally nowhere. We got a star with a number and no habitable planets for light-years. Naw, we're safe because I can finally tell you my news without digital ears catching wind."

"You win the Grand Colonial Lottery or something?" Chuck teased, leaning against the fridge in Lou's kitchen.

His friend shooed Chuck away and opened the fridge door. Rather than the anticipated beer, he pulled out a bottle of champagne. "Not yet. But this'll be close."

Showmanship rarely dazzled a showman. "C'mon, Lou. Spit it out. Or at least lemme hit the washroom quick."

"Robert Ventura has a collection of rare, *original* Earth artwork."

Chuck rolled his eyes and headed for where he knew the *Rex Piscis* had a washroom. "Lou, I know where this is going. But I'm a talker, not a cat burglar. These rich art aficionados all buy top-of-the-line security systems, but they haven't gotten sophisticated enough that I can make friends and swindle the codes out of them." He opened the door and stepped inside.

Thunk.

Breathing a sigh of relief, Chuck took a leak.

Muffled through the door, Lou kept on badgering. "What would you say if I knew a disgruntled employee of the security company that installed Ventura's system?"

Chuck paused mid-stream. "How disgruntled?"

"Fired whistleblower."

Chuck blew a whistle of his own. He finished up and opened the washroom door. "Sure it's not a setup?"

"That's where you come in. I need a team, and I know you're not a thief, but you'd make one *hell* of a recruiter. Wanna help me clear out a *petit Louvre* and fence the haul to an Earth museum for more than we could get on the black market?"

There was only one response Chuck could think of: "*Oui, oui, mon ami.*"

———

Brad knew he should have called it quits and headed back to the *Radio City* before he got caught shopping instead of drifting along at the helm in the midst of the convoy. Technically, Dad hadn't told him he couldn't hang out at the swap meet. But the implicit threat to Brad's bank account—which Dad believed to be non-existent—had made the message clear enough.

Still, two amethysts probably worth an atmospheric hover apiece were burning a hole in his pocket. Not that Brad expected to get anything close to fair market value for them; he doubted Mort had paid full price—possibly any price—wherever they came from. It was more that they currently existed in an unspendable state, and that lack of fungibility gnawed at him.

None of that meant that Brad kept on task the whole time aboard the *Convoy Queen*.

He ate a meal of lobster pot stickers. Not a bit of which was probably as advertised, but it still hit the spot.

He played a few passes of craps at a two-table casino set up between a scarf shop and a guy selling pet rodents.

He turned down the services of four sex workers, only one of which made him think twice.

He hit up an antiques dealer who didn't deal in loose, cut gems. If Brad had the statue or crown or necklace his amethysts came from, maybe the guy would have made him an offer, he said.

He gawked at aftermarket holo-projectors, set up and looping rad-looking scenes from action holos. Man, he would have loved to upgrade the unit on the *Radio City*, but Dad would find some way to fuck him over for flashing that kind of cash without forewarning—not to mention needing to let installers aboard the family ship with no one around to supervise.

He found a guy who was just boldly advertising his services as a fence. Possibly the wisest crook Brad had ever met, the erstwhile planetside pawnbroker wanted nothing to do with Brad's gems. "Listen, kid. Hide those things and take 'em to the core. Turn 'em in for a reward. Someone must own 'em. Anyone who *could* pay you what those are worth would sooner kill you for 'em."

Discouraged—but not willing to heed the fence's warning— Brad wandered aimlessly until a peculiar cadence caught his ear.

"Much value; many shopping," a laaku voice shouted. It sounded like Jomek's dad, Oblek. Given the accent, it would have been hard for it to be anyone else. Most laaku grew up in an English-first school system. Oblek's weird Old-Phabian dialect had rubbed off on Jomek, making them sound weirdly dumb, when in fact they were both biological computers with four hands.

Brad cut over an aisle and tuned his ears to that voice until it came again, like a scanner ping on passive mode.

"All the value; have dealing with me for easy and comfort. Laaku values in deepest space, yes?"

Tacking a course against the flow of shoppers, Brad homed in.

"Discounted coins; small expensive for digital. Best dealing; all sales are desperate!"

When the crowd parted, and he saw his laaku nomad friends, Brad broke into a grin. "Hey, welcome home!" he called out with a wave.

From behind the table where the family was displaying a variety of mysterious electronic devices, Jomek's head popped up. He spotted Brad in an instant. "Renewed friendship, Bradley! Decrease distance; more conversing."

Brad accepted the invitation and strutted over to their little shop. When he made a move to circle around the table for a more casual greeting with his friends, Oblek put up a hand.

When Brad stopped, Oblek pointed to the public walkway. "Public side." Then to the floor beside him. "Business side."

It occurred to him to present the amethysts for appraisal as a pretense for making this a business visit. But he knew the laaku family wasn't into jewel buying—at least not without the promise of obscene profit—and he wasn't looking to flash the purple stones just to win a minor argument.

Thrusting his hands deeper into his jacket pockets, Brad stayed put. "How's the flying?"

"Very good," Oblek answered on behalf of the family. "Few obstructions. Several salvage."

Brad made a show of browsing their wares. It looked like someone had gutted a computer like a fish and splattered the innards as a trophy. "I can see that. How long you been aboard?"

Jomek snickered. "Time is outside. Inside, one day." At the back of the little shop, Jomek's mom, Fooshri, looked up from the circuit board she was soldering and joined her son's mirth. "But without humor, seventy-seven hours eleven minutes."

Brad took a head count. "If you're all here, who's flying?"

"We have very docking," Oblek reported somberly.

Brad blinked.

Oblek couldn't keep a straight face and burst out laughing. "Such laaku a look on your face now! So much belief."

"I could see Brad in mourning of terras lost," Jomek added between giggles. "We are so poor now we are destitute. Please feed us."

Fooshri managed better than her menfolk to maintain her

composure. "We have autodock. *Otoko Feth* drifts happy." She produced a datapad and turned it to face Brad. In Ventura Convoy, anything that tried to transmit beyond the range of the cluster of ships cost a fortune in access fees, so Brad wasn't surprised when the display showed a map of the convoy ships with *Otoko Feth* highlighted.

"How long you gonna be here?" Brad inquired. "You know, since you're not going bankrupt on docking fees?"

"There is a long answer that is better," Jomek began, adding a preamble where none was required. "But the short answer is that here we need to sell our goods; here is the where no one is looking."

"Salvage..." Brad said, nodding along.

"Very legitimate," Oblek insisted deadpan. Then the laaku patriarch winked.

Brad hooked a thumb toward the wild, untamed lands of the swap meet. "Hey, if you're not going anywhere for a while, can I borrow Jomek for some fun?"

"Oh. I could not," Jomek said with a shake of his head. He lowered his voice and shielded his mouth with a hand. "Statistical aberration. Unfortunate debt. We race the compound interest with several haste. All of the urgent."

Brad winced. There were four deadly forces of the cosmos known to spacers: gravity, radiation, magic, and compound interest.

"Well, if you pull ahead in the race, we'll probably be around the next day or two," Brad told the family.

As he walked away, feeling pity for the debt they were struggling to repay, Brad couldn't help brainstorming ways he could help them out.

None of his ideas were remotely legal.

It was a deep-space docking, right there in the midst of Ventura Convoy. Happened all the time. Someone probably kept track of which ships performed the two-airlock mambo, but anyone sorting through that data would have been hard-pressed to draw any conclusions. From old friends catching up to complete strangers conducting one-off business and everywhere in between, the only thing more suspicious than docking was *not docking*.

Chuck waited with Lou, each casually leaning against opposite walls just outside the *Rex Piscis's* airlock. As a live performer, there was a certain energy that audiences expected. While each spectator merely filled a seat, Chuck had to inflate his persona to occupy the entirety of the stage.

With illicit dealings, there was a line to be drawn. At times, it demanded that same pomp and bombast. Mostly, it was a watch-and-see attitude that kept nomads alive in the Black Ocean.

There was a hiss, and Chuck's ears and the door both popped at once when a slightly unequal pressure evened out between ships.

Lou pulled the circular airlock door open with a grunt.

Their visitor came aboard with hands up casually, like a bank robbery hostage in a community theater production. "Heyo, nice to finally meet in the flesh." He was mid-thirties, affable, and relaxed, with stubble and a ponytail that couldn't agree on the color of his hair. The tiniest of shader lenses could have possibly contained data displays or just been a fashion accessory. On his hip, a light-powered blaster rested in a well-worn holster.

"Chuck Ramsey, Joe Johansson."

Chuck offered the requisite handshake. "Is that Jojo... Hansen or Joe... Johansson?"

The new guy cracked a smile. "Second one. Lou musta already told you, but everyone thinks he's a comedian."

"Everyone needs a day job—or in this case, mostly a night job."

"Enough with the small talk," Lou snapped, clearly champing at the bit over this whole business. "Joe, what can you tell us?"

Joe cleared his throat. Chuck squinted subtly as he tried to read a backstory into every mannerism. Something about that *ahem* of his felt academic... like something Mort or a wizard might do before launching into some pedantic rambling or another. "Well, everyone knows Robert Ventura is a class A miserable sonovabitch."

"Granted."

"Yeah. Sums up what I've heard."

"OK, well, here's the thing. As tight as he is with his terras... cheap air filtration, xeno security force that works for food, fiver-and-tennering us for every take-it-for-granted amenity, using—"

"Cut to the chase," Lou said, putting up his hands. "We know he's a goddamn miser. What's the deal with the artwork?"

Chuck cocked a head as he regarded his old friend. "One of your kids on fire or something? What's the caffeine with you?"

"Opportunity doesn't knock. It taps on the door and runs like hell."

"It's the security updates," Joe stated bluntly. "Ventura's missing a patch for a recently discovered exploit."

Chuck burst out laughing, then blew a sigh that flapped his lips. "So... what? We're counting on this guy slacking on his security protocols? What if today's the day his computer gal gets around to tidying up old security holes? Huh? We got a plan for basic fucking computer bookkeeping?"

Lou looked to Joe, then jerked his head at Chuck. "You wanna explain it?"

Joe shrugged. "I got let go. Iron Moon zapped me. But it wasn't exactly out of a moonless night. And before I left, I tagged a few accounts—some of the shadier clients we served—with a future version number of our product."

Folding his arms, Chuck let his blank expression convey his lack of comprehension.

"How can I explain this for a layman...? The system checks against a central databank? Company's got a newer version on file than the one the installed system sees, the databank feeds them the latest and greatest. If not, it gives the old thumbs-up and carries on. But what I did was tell Ventura's system that it was three patches later than it really was. And now, for *two* patches, it's been falling behind and thinking it was ahead."

"Why now? Why not first thing? Why wait for two patches to go by without hitting this ripe, juicy, vulnerable system? Huh? Answer me *that*, and maybe I'm in."

Chuck didn't so much disbelieve the guy as much as he wanted to hear his rationale. A guy who couldn't either think on his feet or prepare to the nines ahead of time wasn't worth partnering for any venture, let alone a heist.

"First patch wasn't for anything that would have made it possible to break past the system. Minor stuff. Glitches. Bugs. Every computer in the galaxy's riddled with 'em. But not all of them are game-breakers. Second one, though... that's what we're looking for. There's a way to send the system into an open-lock crash state without throwing a fault."

It was Chuck's turn to clear his throat.

"Right. Layman. I can use a bug Iron Moon fixed that Ventura doesn't have yet. It'll cause the system to unlock everything and not set off an alarm."

"You people did shitty work," Chuck commented dryly.

Lou backhanded him in the shoulder.

"What? It's true. Big outfit like Iron Moon's got one job: secure stuff. If they don't do that much, what use are they? Not complaining. Joey-boy here got zapped. And we're gonna make a mint on the black market, I presume."

"That's the idea," Lou replied with a nod.

"Sounds good to me," Chuck said. "What exactly are we stealing, and what's the back-alley retail on it?"

"That's the thing," Joe said. "We don't know for sure. Step one is getting someone into Ventura's inner offices and appraise the collection."

Lou leveled a finger at Chuck. "This is where you come in. You know everyone. Who can we get on short notice who could get into that office and ID some oil and canvas?"

Chuck set his jaw and rubbed his chin. "How famous are these paintings?"

This Joe character had such a dead seriousness in his manner Chuck almost wished he hadn't been teasing. For Lou to be this worked up, they had to be big-time. "We can open any flatpic gallery from the omni and play match-the-painting. We're talking Earth art. Stuff with known names. Renaissance, impressionist, pop art. The hard part's going to be setting up a meeting with him. Ideas?"

Oh, Chuck had someone in mind already. "What's Ventura's taste in women?"

———

Brad was preparing himself mentally to give up. Giving up meant that he'd be forced to stash the amethysts on the *Radio City*, abandon his plans to get Jomek and his family out of debt, and go back to roaming from comedy gig to comedy gig at the mercy of whatever colonial yahoos decided Chuck Ramsey was their idea of funny.

To be fair, the latter was his fate anyway unless he ran away from home. But he'd come aboard the *Convoy Queen* with one plan, added a second along the way, and come up with vacuum on both.

Lost in his own head, Brad still had the instincts of a nomad. Someone in the mass of roving sentient life touring the swap meet bumped into him. It wasn't a light bump, nor was it enough to knock him around. One might even say it was perfectly calibrated to distract him without being violent enough to provoke a fight.

Knowing what to watch out for, Brad noticed the hand slip in and out of the front pocket of his jeans.

It was a clean whiff from the pickpocket, since Brad knew better than to keep anything more valuable than candy unsecured on his person.

Instantly finding himself with a clear-cut course of action, Brad whirled and slipped into the flow of shoppers heading the opposite direction. Eyes older than a fourteen-year-old ought to own scanned for a suspect.

Not the brawny spacer with the bicep tattoo.

Not the two women wearing swimsuit tops in the sweltering heat—though Brad checked thoroughly.

Not the guy carrying a tray of nachos and two nearly full beers, navigating the crowd like a champ.

That one.

Trench coat. Hood. Slender. Right distance away for when the impact occurred.

Brad fell into step trailing the mystery pickpocket.

It wasn't as if he was particularly offended. He'd been robbed with threats, at knifepoint, at blasterpoint. But he'd never been pickpocketed as far as he'd ever noticed. For one thing, kids' pockets were a small, low target, and it was easier to rob them with force. This meant that Brad wasn't the only one who considered him grown-up. The galaxy's thieves were catching on.

Brad's would-be robber slipped through the crowd with grace and ease, and despite not getting a look at a face, he updated his description to guess it was a woman.

Not an idiot either. Brad couldn't match his target's speed through the swap meet without jostling and awkward dodges that drew unwanted attention.

"Hey." "Sorry." "Watchit!" "My bad." "Look where you're going." "*You* look where I'm going."

It wasn't long before his pickpocket was actively evading him.

Brad wasn't a big guy. He hadn't grown into his frame. Hadn't bulked up or worked out or started taking pharma like a lot of guys. Nor was he armed. Coming into a potential conflict as the presumed aggressor was a new feeling.

It felt wrong.

Hormones that told him to feel powerful, to scare this pickpocket, to assert dominance, heard a cold, rational voice.

Don't get into a fight you can avoid. You only get to lose one fight, but you can talk your way out of a million jams.

In Dad's philosophy, any fight had the potential to be life or death, and the loser didn't get to decide which. This chase was asking to corner a wary thief. Stealing and carrying a weapon were both crimes on the *Convoy Queen*, and who was to say where this criminal drew a line? Brad's course of action was driving them toward a confrontation he might not walk away from.

Of course, it didn't occur to Brad in the heat of the moment to let things slide. He'd made up his mind. He wanted to know who felt he was a target. Deep down, he wanted to understand why.

Instead of chasing, Brad reviewed the path they'd taken.

Up one aisle of the swap meet, down the next. A simple serpentine route. Thorough, uncreative, and perfectly predictable. If the thief had planned to simply evade Brad through better navigation of the crowded space, it would have been fine.

Brad doubled back. He switched from one flow of humans and xenos to another and headed the opposite direction. Overhead, a sitharn with a blaster rifle peered down from the catwalks. Some help the *Convoy Queen's* security was. Brad had no idea what the trigger would be for them to squeeze off a shot at the shoppers, but he imagined the panic that would ensue and figured they were going to let a lot of offenses go overlooked.

When Brad reached the end of his aisle, he cut through an open stall where racks of women's apparel left mini-paths to shorten his travels. Down the next aisle, he put himself on an intercept course for the thief.

He slowed.

There was no race now. Alertness mattered, not speed.

Tempting though the wares on offer might have been, Brad kept his attention on the people. Far from the tallest among the shoppers, Brad craned and ducked to both keep tabs on his surroundings and not announce his presence to his mark.

When a familiar face appeared, parked in front of a holo-projector showing a loop of what looked like an ancient battle, Brad broke out into a grin. So *this* was how Mort planned to spend his time on the convoy ship.

The wizard's face hung blank, eyes bored, shoulders slack. When the loop finished, he turned to depart the store as a salesman closed in to snag him for a purchase.

Brad spotted his thief. She was thin-faced, with high cheekbones and pale, spacer skin dotted with freckles. Her eyes hid behind a pair of goggles and wispy hair that fell in front of her. She angled toward Mort.

The holovid version played out in Brad's mind.

Mort was an easy mark, distracted and apathetic, off his guard and likely clacking with hardcoin in his pockets. The thief was a shark on the scent of blood in the water. She'd brush against him. Maybe Mort wouldn't notice, and she'd get away with it. More likely, in Brad's mental holotheater, he'd catch her by the wrist, and she'd turn into a newt.

The wizard had been purposely vague when Brad asked exactly what he did to the wizards he hunted. But popular opinion prominently featured unwilling transformations into tiny lizards. While not actually murder, Brad couldn't help thinking the lifespan of the average human trying to live as a newt had to be, like, a day, tops.

He couldn't let that happen.

Shoving and ricocheting through the crowd, Brad rushed past Mort and bowled into the pickpocket, bear-hugging her to keep from either losing her or his balance.

"What the—?"

"Not him!" Brad insisted in a harsh whisper. "Anyone but him!"

When the thief struggled to get free, Brad released her immediately. She had the sense to keep her voice down as sitharn guards congregated above. "Who the fuck do you think you are?"

"I just saved your life," Brad replied, wondering how true it was.

She cast a glance upward. "They're harmless."

Cold-blooded killers with blaster rifles and no mammalian kinship to give them pause didn't exactly strike Brad as harmless, regardless of the likelihood of them intervening. Brad jerked a head toward the wizard, who winked and headed the other direction. "Not them. Him. C'mon. Take a coffee break. I'm buying."

To Brad's surprise, she followed.

All the way to a tesud couple who'd set up a cafe with six tables, some folding chairs, and a Reddi-Bru coffee machine.

Good to his word, Brad paid for a couple basics and took a seat. He planted the other coffee at the seat across from him, brushing some fast-food wrappers onto the floor to make room.

"I'm Brad," he said as she parked herself at the small table.

He could barely see her eyes behind the goggles, but she scanned their surroundings and the cup before lifting it to her lips. She drank and didn't seem bothered by what, by the scent, was a cheap, totally artificial brew. "Neeta," she muttered into her drink.

Neeta held the cup in two hands. Her skin-tight black gloves looked surgical in the emergency medkit sense, the kind worn when no sterile field was available. But Brad knew better. Those were nearly frictionless, with an extra-grip surface only on the fingertips.

"You a lurker?" Brad asked.

"Fuck you." She took another drink of his coffee.

"Hey, no judgment. Just making small talk."

"What was that shit you were slinging back there? Who was that guy? He didn't look connected."

Brad weighed his words. Secrets were secrets, but some were more secret than others. "He might not look it, but he's a hitter."

Neeta snorted in derisive amusement.

"I shit you not."

"*That* guy? In the raggedy sports sweaty and dungos?

Whoever's farming out to guys like that's better off waiting for old age."

What could he say? That Mort spoke a dozen dead languages and knew all the worst words in each? That he was a bigger fugitive than anyone aboard, and that she was small-time by comparison? That he'd walked away from a skyscraper collapse that Brad would have bet good money he had something to do with causing?

Instead, he shrugged. "Hey, go back there and rob him if you don't believe me."

She drank again, huddled in her trench coat, lost in thought. "Why you even care? You think a cup of coffee and a phony rescue is gonna get me wet? That it? 2T buys a cup of shitty java for a cheap whore?"

Brad sipped, nonplussed by the tough act. "It was 5T. But you must have known that. And it really *is* shitty coffee. We buy the bulk discount stuff, and it's better than this."

"We? Who's we? You got a wife you're trying to cheat on?"

Brad spat his next mouthful back into the cup. "How old you think I am?"

"Twenty-five," Neeta replied without hesitation. "I been around, even if I mostly been right here. The way you talk. That ratty old leather jacket you've had since you were my age." Now Brad was wondering at his assessment of *her*. With exposed skin from her nose to her chin to go by, he'd guessed early twenties for her. "Plus the 'tude. I watched your eyes. You're not following every firm tush that walks by. It's called Ponce. It's new. But *you* already knew that, right?"

"What now?" She'd veered off course and lost him.

"Ponce. Fountain of Youth. It's phony as Neru Meatloaf. Just cosmo in a pill. Mostly a girlie drug, but you creepers have caught on."

Brad pushed his chair back. "Whatever, sister. You're

welcome for the coffee. I'm done with my charity work for the month."

Neeta caught Brad by the wrist before he could rise. "Sit." Brad sat, not because she ordered it, or even because she had a grip like an arm-wrestling champ, but because her change in demeanor intrigued him. "You really are a kid, aren't you?"

"I'm a man of limited age but vast experience."

"How limited?"

The instinct to pad the number fell before a wave of earnestness. "Fourteen."

Slumping back in her chair, Neeta folded her arms. "Shiiiit. I'm getting too old for this business if I'm getting made by pre-pubes."

Brad leveled a finger across the table. "Hey, I'm all man."

"Your voice hasn't even changed."

"Has too. You should have heard me before. *I was quite the soprano.*" That was it. His falsetto got a laugh out of her. "But in all seriousness, I'm no kid. Data-pushers back in the core may say so, but you grow up faster out in the Black Ocean."

"Here, you either grow up, or someone grows you up."

Brad didn't need to be told what that meant. She was as much an adult as him, and he didn't need to bother asking her age. Whether she was twelve or twenty, he'd treat her as a peer. And since he already *knew* she was a thief, he had one question he felt compelled to ask.

He leaned across the table and dropped his voice. "So... what's a quick way to earn a load of terras on this barge?"

———

"No."

"Aw, c'mon. You'd be great."

Becky rolled her eyes and put a fist on one hip while

balancing Rhiannon on the other. "Chuck, you're sweeter'n Frosti Pops, but in what galaxy you think I'm the gal for this gig?"

They'd rendezvoused outside the family washroom near the giant cafeteria and found a quiet place near an "employees only" door. Lou leaned against the wall, letting Chuck handle the intra-Ramsey negotiations while Mikey pestered Joe to play restaurant with him.

"This one," Chuck insisted. "Big V is a middle-aged bachelor. He doesn't get around, so he's at the mercy of the convoy for entertainment. Have you looked around? You're hotter than a plasma conduit."

Becky was already shaking her head. "Big cheese like that? Only wants one thing."

Without moving his feet, Chuck leaned toward his wife. "You wouldn't have to uck-fay him," he told her under his breath.

Mikey looked over his shoulder. "Mommy likes to uck-fay."

Chuck's eyes widened. "We need a new code." Lou smirked quietly and kept his opinions to himself.

"No it-shay," Becky snarked back at him. "Cat's out of a few too many bags as it is, though. But that ain't the problem, see? Guy gets himself a pile of moolah, his brain gets a little soggy. He wants 'em easy, and easy means young and dumb. Doubt I got enough giggles left in me to pull that off."

"I have giggles," Rhiannon chimed in, then proceeded to demonstrate.

Chuck turned to his friend. "Lou, can you watch Lucy and Desi while Becks and I have a serious discussion?"

"Sure thing," Lou replied easily. He came over, and Becky passed Rhi to him without a fuss on either side. After all, he was Uncle Lou, a guy she'd known on and off her whole little life. But then Lou just stood there, letting

Rhiannon play with his hair as she perched atop his shoulders.

"Somewhere else?" Chuck added.

"Oh. Sure." Lou jerked his head toward Mikey and Joe. "C'mon, fellas. Let's grab a bite. Uncle Lou's buying."

Once they were gone, Becky donned her best scowl. "It ain't about the sex. It ain't even the crime; this one seems like a nice, easy slag. You get to stay in the background, which is all I ever ask."

"So what's the bag? Why you flaking on this one?"

She knew they needed the moolah. Vega IX had softened them up, gotten them a little used to having money coming in that could go out just as easily. And like she said, this wasn't going to be dangerous from *their* end. Not even the one distracting Ventura would be too exposed—other than literally, in Becky's case.

"Chuck, ain't nobody sees me naked the way you see me naked. Not even me. *Especially* not me."

"How's that, exactly?"

"Like I'm twenty-one, still."

"I'd have said twenty-five. At twenty-one, your curves hadn't finished filling out."

Becky smirked. "If you're fishing for something extra naughty, you're using the right bait. But this ain't about those rose-tinted goggles you got on. Them blurry things've got your name engraved on 'em, and you ain't sharing."

Objectively, Chuck suspected she might be right. After all, what were the odds that his was the only wife in the galaxy who looked hotter after giving birth to four kids, including one old enough to enlist?

At maybe one in a million, it seemed out of keeping with the luck Chuck had been dealt in life.

He huffed a beleaguered sigh. "What now? We're short on

personnel here. Joe's single, and Lou's flying solo while his kids finish a school semester on Carousel. They brought me in to assemble a team, and I'm working with scraps here."

"And the scraps aren't having it?" Becky teased.

"You know what I mean. I'm EV without a suit here."

Becky shrugged. "Dunno what to say. This stuff's your bag. But you don't have a gig lined up or any leads; none you've bothered to mention, anyway. So either you pull in some terras soon, or I'll be standing at an intersection out there in my skivvies until we can afford to put aside enough to make it to the next planet."

"Things aren't *that* tight," Chuck protested. He didn't mind sharing a little love among friends, but even putting her in range of a lecherous convoy CEO didn't sit quite right with him.

She patted his cheek. "Well, don't let 'em *get* that tight. Take a walk. Breathe the vibe. Something'll come to you." There was a twinkle in her eye. "And if you come up with a way that doesn't drag me into whoring for a job, I've got some surprises out of the Emtek Grawl for ya."

Chuck gaped. Most of the stuff out of that laaku recreational sex manual wasn't even possible for humans. On the flip side, Becky wasn't one to make promises she couldn't deliver on.

He gave her a quick kiss. "See, babe? This is why we're a perfect pair."

As Chuck's long strides carried him through the *Convoy Queen*, the shops and stalls and shoppers and hawkers all blurred together into a gestalt. A feel. He entered a sublime state where the universe would open itself and fill his mind with the solution.

A grating voice snapped Chuck from his reverie.

"Hey, Dad!"

This was what he was talking about. This was a real opportunity, not a leaking gig where some outfit drip, drip, dripped terras to you in exchange for labor—or in Dad's case, lame jokes.

"So, how soon'll they be here?" Brad asked, barely able to contain his excitement.

Neeta shrugged. She had a mouth full of barbecue wings anyway. When she swallowed, she ventured a guess. "Maybe a couple days. They're not on anyone's schedule but their own. All I can say is, someone transmitted the convoy location to the Howling Comets, and those guys know better than to bite the hand that pays them."

Pirates. Real, honest-to-God Black Ocean pirates. Dad did a pretty good job steering them clear of deep space buccaneers, but a place like Ventura Convoy was neutral ground. Pirates couldn't sell just anywhere, and if they wanted to save for cushy retirement, they needed to convert plunder to terras.

After all, no one died of old age as a working pirate. All those magnificent bastards had an exit plan—or at least came up with one when their bones started to creak.

"And they're really gonna be that careless?"

"Arrogant," Neeta corrected. She wiped her mouth with the heel of her hand and her hand on her pants. "It's not like they don't *care*; it's that they can't be bothered to keep databases on everything. They get what they got, then just come spray it. Collect terras. Simple pimple."

"What if we get caught?"

Neeta pushed back her chair. "Why you gotta ask that? No one wants that. Not us. Not *them*. They don't want trouble. Not here. It's like puking at the dinner table. Maybe you can just say you gotta, but it makes everyone oogie. And it's embarrassing. And if it happens, it's gonna be all the yak around this sector for years."

"How many you think you can get hired?"

This was the real question. Even with the two of them on the job, they'd be limited as to how much they could cart off before anyone noticed. Unless the Howling Comets scored a lucky stash of data crystals or some lucrative pharma, getting paid for real on this one relied on bulk transport. Bulk transport meant grav sleds, hover-carts, musclebound xenos, or all of the above.

"It's a popular hustle," Neeta hedged as she got up from the table. "Three? Five. Odd numbers are lucky."

Brad frowned slightly. "You for real, or are you just eating while I'm buying?"

"Fine. You want two and four on the table? Have 'em. But you want in on this, you gotta match me one for one. And just us two won't cut it." She looked him up and down, and the implication was clear: Brad wasn't the "hauling shit" kind of guy.

"I can get some muscle."

"Not just muscle. *Smart* muscle. For every hauler, you need a skimmer to pass off to. They need to be quick to spot transfer orbits."

"We're still talking about *on ship*, right?"

"Yeah. Figure of speech. And the real reason we want an odd number is so someone is left as lookout and comms."

Comms? Bitchin'! That meant someone would be coordinating through earpieces, watching the whole operation, and running it like an orbital traffic controller.

"Well, time for me to hold up my end of the deal," Brad declared.

Neeta followed him as he got up and headed for the

corridor that would lead to the docking airlocks. "Wait. Don't you want me to tell you how—?"

"Nope," Brad replied curtly. "Team first, then details. You gotta plan around who you get, and the sooner we know the team, the sooner we can tailor a plan."

This was it. This was his big break. Who cared if he fenced the amethysts at this point? This was a score he'd brag about years from now. Robbing pirates? How would women resist after they heard that one?

Plus, this sounded like the perfect opportunity to rope Jomek and his parents into a job that would get them out of debt.

As he was formulating his pitch for the laaku family, Brad spotted an even easier route to solving the recruitment puzzle.

"Hey, Dad!" He raised a hand and waved to catch his father's attention.

Multiple heads turned at his shout. Brad supposed widespread fatherhood made that a common nickname.

"What are you doing?" Neeta whisper-yelled at him. "You're drawing attention."

The grin on his face wouldn't budge. "Attention is innocuous. But bringing him into this is step one."

Chuck Ramsey was going to eat Brad's ions. *He* had come up with a way to earn some real terras for the family.

———

"No."

"Seriously, kid, I've got a real thing going here."

Chuck couldn't believe his ears. How long had the kid been angling for a score? Months? No. Years? That didn't even seem to cut it. Bradley Carlin Ramsey had been an aspiring conman before since he'd been a cluster of cells in the womb.

Brad grabbed him by the sleeve and yanked him aside. Lou and Joe smirked from the sidelines as the girl watched inscrutably from behind those goggles. It wasn't like the kid was strong. Maybe a little stronger than Chuck had prepared for; strong enough that he'd caught his old man unawares and drawn a stumble that he'd been forced to parlay into following along rather than fall on his face.

From point-blank range, albeit from 20 cm below, Brad snarled at him through gritted teeth. "I found a job for us. Me. Through her. You're not roping her into whatever laseroid mess of a plan you cooked up. Especially not as bait."

"Not bait. Distraction. And I'm only looking for a distraction because your mom won't play ball this time."

"Nice..." Brad replied, bobbing his head as if he didn't mean that at all. "There are some things a guy doesn't need to hear about his mom. Like how his dad whores her out for jobs."

"It's not whoring, just teasing. I don't think giving it up would give us a large enough window. Lecherous old autocrats aren't known for being skilled or considerate lovers."

"No."

"Maybe we should ask *her*. Huh? How about a little empowerment awareness on your part? I didn't raise you to impose your—"

"No. That's final. Why are you so hung up on this, anyway?"

Desperation. Chuck answered in his head and kept it there. If he couldn't pull a crew together on short notice, Joe and Lou would find someone who could. And while he was in the business of being quietly honest with himself between verbalized lies: who even knew if the person under all that obscuring fabric was the kind who could play the part? After all, even in the middle of nowhere, a rich fucker probably had *some* standards.

"Fine. You wanna pitch a better job. Take the floor." Chuck backed away from his son and swept a theatrical arm toward his business partners.

Brad paused, understandably wary of the offer. Chuck hadn't raised an idiot. An asshole, maybe, but not an idiot. Taking a deep breath, the boy nodded. "Low risk, high reward. It's an instant inside job. There's a major incoming shipment, and they're going to be hiring temp help to unload it all."

"What kind of shipment?" Lou asked, playing along.

"Assorted," Brad replied smoothly, which was a nice way of saying he was clueless. "We won't know until they start unloading."

Chuck sensed it coming. He knew Lou would pick up on it, but Joe got there first. It was a sniper's question, lined up and deadly as soon as someone pulled a trigger. "Who exactly is... 'they'?"

After all, the other plan was Joe's baby. He had a pride stake in its success even if they came up with another avenue to easy riches.

It was the girl who answered. "Howling Comets." There were gasps and tongue-swallowings throughout the gathering; Chuck practically spat out a beverage he wasn't drinking. "This is neutral ground. They're not looking for a fight. Two... three times a year, they stop off, unload their shit. No one complains where it came from; no one gets hurt. Plenty goes missing, and no one cares."

"No one cares...?" Chuck echoed dubiously.

The new girl huffed. "Fine. People care. Just not the pirates. It's a dogpile getting the gig. We got more worries getting re-boosted than the pirates deciding to take up accounting."

Lou shook his head. "Sounds like a load of trouble."

Chuck joined him. It was a joint head-shaking operation. "We've got a bigger score lined up with fewer risk factors."

"Mind telling us precisely *what* we're competing against here, Professor Moriarty?" Brad asked deadpan, name-dropping a villain he'd learned from a paper book, no doubt.

The real question wasn't whether he trusted his boy to be cool with the info. This was a prelude to bringing him in on a big score. Potential downside: getting his boy hooked on a life of crime instead of allowing nature to take its course and absolve him of direct responsibility. Potential upside: making a good case for two shares of the split, with both of them essentially coming to him since Brad was too young to open a solo bank account.

Whether the girl was to be trusted... Well, she was no bigger risk than Joe at this point.

"Ventura's art collection."

Neeta snorted. "Good luck. No one gets in there. Private gallery."

Chuck leveled with her. "That's why we were looking to get someone very 'private' invited to see it."

Brad piped up. "Who *does* get in? Can't be literally no one."

Little Miss Trenchcoat paused before answering. "I don't keep tabs, but I know he's had security installers in there... art dealers... appraisers... at least one guy from a megacorp trying to buy from him..."

Brad snapped his fingers. "That's it."

Chuck hated that. Kid came up with off-the-cuff shit too readily, and too little of it was viable. "What's 'it'?"

"We need an art buyer, not a whore."

Trenchcoat cleared her throat. "I can *find* us a prossy; you'll still want to keep Big-V busy."

"Where are we going to find an art buyer on this boat?"

Chuck demanded testily. Oh, yeah. Nice call. Let's just conveniently have a highly specialized professional available at the push of a button. "Anyone who could afford to buy from Ventura would have commed ahead."

Brad smirked the smirk that Chuck always wanted to smack off his face. At times, his 'no child abuse' pact with Becky was a real drag. "What if the buyer isn't the sort who uses comms?"

"I don't get it," Joe interjected.

Chuck did. Chuck got it hard. "What's he even know about art?"

The kid knew enough not to drop names before anything was really on the table. "Oh, lemme guess... snooty Earth education with the accent to match. Thinks quick on his feet. Doesn't get flustered. Even if he doesn't know every painting or statue—"

Joe shot up a warning hand. "We're just after paintings. Nothing bulky or heavy."

Chuck shook his head. "He wouldn't do it, anyway. This isn't his game."

Brad rubbed his temples. He blew a frustrated breath. "Don't you *get it? He's. Bored.*"

"Bored?" Chuck echoed. How did a guy who could sit quietly, purportedly playing both sides of a game of chess in his head, get bored?

"Yeah. He's moping around the swap meet, window shopping. That's how Neeta and I met. I saved her life when she was thinking of picking his pocket."

"He'd never have noticed," Neeta grumbled.

Brad turned to her. "And that slim chance was the thread you dangled your life from."

"Who're they talking about?" Joe demanded.

"That the hitchhiker you dragged to Carson?" Lou asked.

Chuck thought about it. If they needed someone to play a snooty art connoisseur from Earth, they could hardly hope to do better. The trick was selling the heist as a lark. "His name's Mort. And if he's in, I think we've got ourselves a heist."

The utter variety of foods that were available impaled upon a plastic skewer never ceased to amaze. Mort had only recently deemed the deep-fried hotdog on a stick digested enough to chance another culinary adventure. Now he stood in an aisle of the swap meet trying to choose between the stall peddling caramel-apples-on-a-stick and the stranger-but-possibly-healthier cart touting salad-on-a-stick.

"Hey, there you are!" a youthful voice announced as greeting.

Setting aside a decision that would no doubt prove inadvisable in retrospect no matter the outcome, Mort turned around to see Brad coming up fast. His companion was the scrawny wisp in the trench coat that he'd just about tackled earlier that afternoon.

Unable to resist adding a bit of casual pedantry, he replied, "Been where I am since before I was born. No truer and few more useless words have ever been uttered."

The trench coat spoke with a young woman's voice, nasal and piqued. "You're right. He is kinda Earthy on the ears."

Mort harrumphed. "I'd thank you to reserve your disparaging comments for private conversation."

"I didn't! I'm being totally paraging here!" Brad proclaimed. He got right up close, close enough that a younger lad might have grabbed an arm or a sleeve and learned a valuable lesson. But Brad wasn't that big a fool, and the size he was happened to be a different sort entirely. "Can we go somewhere out of the way?"

"Whose way?"

"Is he always like this?" the trench coat girl asked.

"Yeah," Brad replied readily. "He's perfect."

"Why do I gather that I'm about to hear the details of some rare opportunity that I'd be a fool to pass up?"

Brad grinned. "Because you're smart. Neeta, can you lead us someplace secluded?"

Mort gazed around. "Seclusion is quite the commodity around here. Can we afford the rates?"

"One of the perks of living here. I know the quiet places."

A shrewd one by her manner, Mort gave Brad's companion the once-over. She stood in the middle ground between wizard and troublemaker in height; shoes instead of boots, so the measure ought to have been accurate. At that size and with no gravel to the voice, he judged the girl full-grown but not remotely old. She belonged in high school or college, he estimated, not graduate school. Every feature but her mouth and chin hid behind the simplistic costume of coat, hood, goggles, and gloves. Her scent spoke of infrequent hygiene, and her bearing projected a squirrelly paranoia. Then again, good posture and clear diction despite the grubby accent suggested an education and family.

In short, she was a local, an in-between, but not born to the life. If nothing else, she seemed sharp as shattered glass, and he ought to at least go along to limit the trouble Brad got himself into.

"Fine. Lead on."

Mort had expected the shipboard equivalent of a back alley or a broom cupboard. Instead, Brad's friend led them to what appeared to be a faculty break room, albeit decorated with the spare and industrial style of an indigent science-repairman.

Brad and the girl took seats on crates that slid up to a collapsible table with a hollow scrape that suggested emptiness. Long having given up pretension, Mort dragged forth a container labeled as once containing household medical supplies.

"Mort, Neeta. Neeta, this is Mort. He's a wizard."

"So, we're going around telling people that, these days?" Mort inquired, raising an eyebrow. He gazed at Neeta. "Were you aware of the risk to which he's subjecting you?"

"I've dealt with dangerous people before."

Despite his annoyance, he couldn't help admiring the boldness. "I'll hear you out. What's going on that involves your new friend?"

"Actually, it's one of Dad's ideas," Brad preambled.

"That's a horrid way to begin a sales pitch."

Brad put up his hands. "I know. I know. But we're going full-honesty mode here. Complete disclosure. Dad's putting together a crew for a heist."

Mort burst out laughing. "Let me guess. *I'm* the muscle?"

Without hesitating, Neeta fired off with, "I don't think we're *that* desperate for muscle." She sized him up, perhaps noting that as far as literal muscle, Mort left something to the imagination.

"It's a no-muscle job. Even *Mom* is kinda OK with it."

Mort rubbed his chin. For the first time, he found genuine curiosity edging past the morbid sort. "Go on. What's the job?"

"Guy who runs the convoy, Ventura, he's a dick and a half. Got a collection of stolen Earth art aboard. Real stuff. Like, painted on caves practically."

"Not painted on caves. On canvas," Neeta clarified.

"But people can't just waltz in and look around. It's private. Need to be a friend or an art dealer or shit to see it."

"That's where you dock, apparently," Neeta added with a shrug.

"Befriend the owner of the ship?" Mort inquired, still not quite sure of the role they wanted him to play here.

"No. You get to pose as an art buyer." Brad's grin said this was supposed to be the role of a lifetime, an opportunity to live out a long-standing dream.

"Pass."

"WHAT?"

"You said he'd—"

"I know what I said. Mort, how can you not want in? Priceless paintings. Once we fence them, they go back to snooty museums in Sol. Probably even Earth. We make like an entire escape pod stuffed with terras and do the art world a favor in the process."

"Never cared for the art world."

"But—"

"And what do I know about art? Bunch of mustache-waxing, tweed-hearted ninnies peering through monocles at the brain excrement of a mostly deranged class of creative vagabonds."

Brad aimed an accusing finger back the way they'd come, back toward the swap meet and its gloriously nonsensical commerce. "You'd really rather go back to browsing techno back-scratchers, fried stick-food, and a million gizmos to have sex without another person involved? *That's* what you'd pick over getting rich with us?"

The boy was growing into a natural speech-maker. Harvard might have turned him into a decent debater, even if he'd never had a shot at getting into Oxford. Even knew to use some wizardly slang for science contraptions.

And more than that, the boy had a valid point. What else *was* he doing? Crime might not have been a standard solution to ennui, but who the hell cared at this point? Mort wasn't beholden to anyone but himself. He could flout the laws of nature, man, or demon if he chose.

"Fine. I'm in."

———

Renting a function room was the sort of bold, they'd-never-think-to-look-there thinking that the planner of any good heist relied on. If this all painted by the numbers, no one would even come looking for them, let alone analyze their recent activities to piece together a roster of who'd been involved.

Chuck was pretty proud of himself for thinking of it.

"There," Fooshri declared as she thumped an access panel back into place with a lower hand. "Zero peeking. Even less listening. Our actions contain themselves."

Lou peered over the laaku's shoulder as if he knew the second thing about covert surveillance equipment or how to bypass it. "No offense, but how can you be sure you got all of them?"

Oblek snickered. "Very smart one I got. She is the expert of the small things. I am the tinker of large things. We are a match made in advanced engineering graduate program."

Fooshri shook her head. "The saying does not work in Human."

"Works well enough," Joe commented dryly as he pulled up a chair to the long, wobbly table the room provided. "How about we get everyone acquainted? We all need to know the plan inside out, and that includes knowing who's doing what."

Chuck took the floor—and the head of the table. "Have a seat, everyone. Coffee's gratis, but I can't recommend it. We'll send out for food as we go. Let's go around and tell everyone who we are and why we're each here. Aliases are kosher. Not looking to run background on Ventura's omni. Just need a name to call you by."

"Can we get cool nicknames?" Brad piped up. "If so, I call dibs on Maverick."

Chuck paused a moment to consider. "Probably not a bad idea. You can give us a name, but everyone pick a sobriquet. No need to broadcast ID during a job like this. Lou, get us started."

Lou pushed back his chair and stood, wringing his hands. "Uh. I'm Lou Williams. I'm a trader. Picked up an oil printer when I heard about this job, so I'll be providing the forgeries we swap in."

"Getting ahead of ourselves," Chuck butted in. "Just the basics."

"Oh. Fine. Well, for this one, call me... I dunno, van Gogh."

Joe shook his head. "No good. Nothing art related. Don't want to confuse you with a painter when we're talking about the goods."

"Right. Sorry. Hold on. Lemme think..."

"We'll come back to you. Brad, go ahead."

Brad tipped his chair back. "I'm Chuck's oldest. Pilot, fast-talker, crack shot with a blaster. Consider me a wild card; I can do whatever needs doing. And like I said, I'm taking Maverick."

"Yeah, yeah," Chuck grumbled. "And anyone under the age of thirty here is on lookout duty."

Brad pinwheeled his arms as his outrage verged on overbalancing his teetering chair. "WHAT? No fair!"

"Young eyes are excellent eyes," Jomek commented. "I am young and a lookout. I am Jomek, but for this arrangement, I will be Opko."

"I won't remember that," Lou griped.

"Famous laaku astronomer," Oblek explained. "Much math. Very orbital."

"Copernicus," Mort sniped from the far side of the table.

"The human who lassoed the planets of Sol. Sounds like the two-handed equivalent of yours."

"Acceptable," Jomek agreed.

Chuck aimed a finger at Oblek, and the laaku stood on his chair. "I am Oblek of Phabian. I am the mechanic. The trader." He glanced over at his wife and let his voice grumble slightly. "The... lover."

"Name," Chuck prompted deadpan as Oblek and Fooshri made doe eyes at one another.

"Blessed loin-minder, what's the word for *gheruse*?" Oblek asked.

Fooshri scratched her scalp with a bare lower hand. "Cucumber. I think."

"Good enough," Chuck declared. "How about you?"

Fooshri didn't hesitate. "Handkerchief."

"Great," Chuck replied, not even caring. He'd known Oblek and Fooshri since before he'd met Becky, and there were times where their cultural oddities growing up outside mainstream, humanophilic society were just beyond him. "Joe?"

"I'm the one with the security bypasses that make this venture anything more than a pleasure-pod daydream. Call me Ishmael."

Chuck cracked a smirk. It was an old joke. As a purveyor of old jokes himself, Chuck suspected Joe was tipping a cap to the one who'd pulled together a crew for his job.

That only left one member of the team, the one Chuck—unbelievably—had the least confidence in. And that was with Brad and Jomek involved. "Neeta?"

Huddled in that dusty old trench coat, Neeta didn't perk up from her slouch or uncross her arms. "I live in the pipes. I know the 'timers. We need something, I find it. We need someone, I make an intro."

Chuck knew the slang well enough to realize that the pipes bit might or might not have been literal. Typically, it was just a reference to camping out in the machinery of a ship or station instead of a room with a bed.

"We still need that distraction," Joe pointed out.

"You'll get your prossy," Neeta promised. "I know a bunch. I'll front. Not adding a split for a little back work. Deep kosher?"

Lou shook his head. "Nah. Not yet. I wanna look you in the eye. I'm a handshake man, and I believe in looking a new business associate square in the eye."

Neeta looked to Brad for support, but the boy shrugged. She checked with Chuck, but he circled a finger for her to speed things along. This wasn't a heist with a personnel department. If it took the mildest of privacy invasions to keep everyone calm and cooperative, Chuck was for it. Sensing a blockade with no other way around, the girl complied.

Because when Neeta pushed up her goggles and let her hood fall back, it was clear she was young enough to be his daughter. Her eyes were red-rimmed and bloodshot, with pale irises that suggested either a genetic aberration or some weird cosmo as a kid. She had a thin face with prominent cheekbones and an indented outline where her goggles habitually rested, cleaner than the rest of her skin.

"Happy?" She glared at Lou, who shrugged.

"Yeah."

"Codename?" Chuck prompted, eager to get beyond the roll call and to the meaty planning of the heist.

"Gremlin."

Chuck clapped his hands together and rubbed them. "Super. You all know me. I'm Chuck Ramsey, heretofore comedian turned heist coordinator. I'll be the voice on the comms. The voice of God. Call me Chaplain. Now, let's all get down to business."

"Um, Chaplain?" Joe asked, hooking a thumb. "Aren't you going to do our art dealer?"

"Oh, him? That's Mort."

Joe shook his head emphatically. "I need more than that. I want to hear from the only guy who's got to interact directly with Ventura. I want to know this job is going to achieve escape velocity."

Chuck flourished a hand, a cue for the wizard to make his own introduction.

With slowness that teetered on the edge between melodrama and menace, Mort rose. He was unshaven and in need of a comb. His sweatshirt looked like it had gotten mangled in a processor years ago and refused to ever be washed again. Yet for all that, every gaze in the room was black-holed onto him.

"The quick version is that I'm a wizard, and a friend of Chuck's, and doing him a favor getting involved here. The long version is a tale of ancient magics and Sol politics, of bargains and oaths kept in spite of dire consequences, of shattered lives and stolen relics. As for my qualifications here, I was born and educated on Earth, come from a notable family, and have dealt with more snot-nosed aristocrats than the lot of you will be cursed to meet in your entire lives."

"Satisfied?" Chuck asked.

Joe boggled. "I think I have more questions now than before."

Mort huffed. "Since, for my cover story, I'm probably going to just use my real identity, I might as well bind you all to keeping the following secret." Before Mort could poll for who'd be willing to bear his secret, he launched right into it. "My name is Mordecai The Brown. I was valedictorian at Oxford,

Eighth Chair of the Convocation Grand Council, and Guardian of the Plundered Tomes. Certain disreputable characters in my ancestry have claimed a direct line of descent from Merlin himself. I choose to believe them.

"When the Convocation had wizards go bad, they'd sent inquisitors to bring them to justice. When they went *particularly* bad, they sent librarians—who worked for me. When I went bad, there wasn't a plan B. Just guessing, but they must be down to plan Q by now, and I'm still sailing the stars free as a vulture. To clarify, I'm not on the run from the law. I'm not even *fleeing* assassins. I kill them as I find them. And if this dilapidated scow weren't held together with spit and popsicle sticks that would shatter if I sneezed hard, I'd take the paintings by force.

"So let's just have a fun heist and not try any funny business."

A stunned silence followed. It lingered after Mort fetched himself a cup of the swill they called coffee around here and sat back down with it.

Brad broke the ice with a cheery reminder. "Mort, you didn't pick a name." Even Chuck didn't want to be the first one to speak after that speech. Never follow an act with a kid or an animal. He amended that list to include wizards.

The Convocation fugitive rolled his eyes. "Mordred. Why not?"

"Alrighty!" Chuck declared. He placed a mini holo-projector at the center of the table. It popped up a 3D map of the *Convoy Queen*. "Let's hammer out a plan!"

―――

OK. Here's the deal. Neeta—dammit, I mean Gremlin—I need you to find who to talk to. We need to get Mort ... no, I refuse to call him that ... fine, arrange Mordred *a meeting with Ventura as a potential buyer with deep pockets.*

Lou—hey, did we ever pick a name for Lou? I don't think we did. Lou, you're Peanut ... yeah, live with it. Peanut, take Mordred and get him cleaned up; shave, new suit, all that jazz.

Mordred... Just walk in like you don't own the place, but you're considering the purchase. ID all the art worth taking and report back.

Lines of expenses and income scrolled past at a precisely calibrated speed that allowed Robert Ventura to absorb the data as quickly as his eyes could handle it. Every terra the convoy interacted with, incoming and outgoing, showed up on the screen: from cash kickbacks reported dutifully by ship personnel to core world investments accruing interest, from lunch tray deposits to pirate tributes.

Today was a good day. High income. No variances. The shoppers were dumb and happy and poured their money into Ventura's coffers.

He watched with shoulders hunched and chin perched on his laced fingers, elbows propped on the glossy black surface of his desk. The data was, to him, the sheet music of a song. He could hear the melody of profit, of prosperity.

A chime from the comm panel beside his ledger screen shattered the tranquility.

"What?" He demanded.

"*It's 3:55. You have a meeting.*" Marie-Ellen never interrupted without reason, and this was no exception. She bore his snippiness without complaint, unlike a long line of predecessors.

With a scowl deepening on his brow, Ventura verified that he had, in fact, lost track of the time. He hastily cleared his thoughts for what might prove to be a pleasant encounter.

It wasn't every day that a deep-pocketed buyer arrived to view his collection.

Normally, Ventura wasn't wont to part with his pride and joy, but shrewd investment had grown the gallery from seedling terras. With occasional trimming and a good harvest of the fruit the grove bore, he could plant new pieces to enjoy even more.

One couldn't allow emotional attachment to interfere with business.

Ventura stretched stiff legs and shrugged into the jacket to his suit. For a moment, he considered a tie, then decided against. He wanted to look like a *successful* businessman, not one beholden to a traditional dress code.

Just before he headed into the gallery, he keyed the desk comm. "Send him in."

Doors at either end of the gallery opened in near-perfect unison. Ventura strode in, beaming pride from his smile. Few among the visitors to his private collection could appreciate the rare beauty on display. A vanishing few could afford it.

Through the opposite door came a stern, slender gentleman of aristocratic bearing, the sort of casual associate of money that could lounge in a ten-thousand-terra suit as if it were a poolside towel. The man's angular face had a set jaw and eyes like mining lasers. His hair was slicked back and glossy with some kind of styling product. A wash of aftershave preceded Ventura's visitor in advance of their handshake.

"Welcome to the Ventura Convoy; I'm Robert Ventura."

"Mordecai The Brown," the visitor identified himself. He had a firm handshake despite bony fingers. He gave the room a quick glance. "Quite an exhibit considering the humility on display throughout the rest of this bloated sardine can."

The wizard's voice rasped like a metal file. If this man was intimidated by money or manpower, he didn't show it in his choice of words.

Nothing could dim Ventura's pride in his art collection, however. He ambled clockwise, allowing his guest to take in the gestalt of the exhibit before they dove into negotiations for individual works.

Each painting perched on a pedestal, boxed in by glassteel, suffocated in nitrogen to prevent degradation. Soft lighting displayed each to its best advantage. Soft music twinkled from overhead speakers localized to a particular soundtrack for each work. Soft carpets cushioned footsteps to keep outside stimuli from interfering with the experience.

"How stolen are these?" Mordecai asked bluntly. "By that, I mean how close are the authorities to tracking them this far?"

"I assure you, the provenance of these pieces has been extensively obfuscated."

Mordecai harrumphed. "If I'm buying anything, I want to know who had it last, when you got it from them, and whether anyone's sniffed around after it since you've had it."

The wizard let his gaze do his browsing as he kicked off the contentious portion of the proceedings almost immediately. Ventura worked to hide his disappointment at not having an appreciative audience.

"Well, this is a piece that went missing during the Vincente Incident in 2192. It turned up in my black-market circles after a three-hundred-year absence in obscurity. I acquired it last year from an eyndar trader who'd purchased it off pirates in Epsilon Sector."

"The Wedding Feast at Cana. Louvre's still pissed about that one. Earthlings might be willing to pay more to get that back than I could pull together."

Ventura snickered. "Last thing I want is a trail connecting me to Earth Interstellar."

Mordecai nodded. "Feel the same about the Convocation."

"Your reputation *does* precede you."

The wizard stopped in his meandering tracks. "My reputation can take a nap and wake up thinking it was all a dream. And you can tell your arcanist lackey to knock off early and smoke a bowl. He'll pop an eye out of its socket if he tries any harder to keep me from working magic."

Ventura smiled to cover the pang of fear in his gut. There had been a known wizard or two aboard the *Convoy Queen*. None had noticed Blanton's efforts and made a stink about it before. "I assure you, it's a standard precaution."

"Standard, schmandard. It's insulting. It's like one of them Gold League xenos getting stopped by a bouncer at the door to a bar. You say you've heard of me. Maybe you haven't heard enough. If I want to work any magic I like, I will. Thus far, I'm respecting the customs of your domain and taking it easy on your hemophilic technology. Don't make me prove a point."

"And if I think you're bluffing?" Ventura countered. He'd heard more bluster in his lifetime than most, and these were the words of a man who knew Ventura didn't *want* to call his bluff.

Mordecai gave a wan smile and dared to put a hand on Ventura's shoulder. "I've seen what I need to see. Raphael, Degas, Magritte, van Gogh, Warhol. Good merchandise. Good use of the terras that seem to follow me around when their previous owners don't need them anymore. How about you start thinking of prices where you'd be willing to part with each. Meanwhile, I'll be enjoying the amenities of one of the rathole hotels you've got set up here—gratis."

"If you're so rich, you can afford to—"

Mordecai cut him off with a raised finger. "Because I can walk away from here with my money and live just fine. If you can't spare the paltry few hundred terras you'd charge me for accommodations when I'm potentially spending upward of half a billion terras, I'll know the kind of businessman you are."

With that, without even being dismissed, Mordecai headed for the exit.

Ventura stood in stunned silence. Had he heard that right? *Half a billion?*

"Is this door going to get out of my way, or am I going to need to open it myself?" The wizard didn't bother looking back.

Ventura rushed over and tapped the door panel; it wasn't as if it were remotely locked from this side. He knew better than to even give the impression of imprisoning a guest, let alone a notorious wizard.

"I'll make sure your every comfort is seen to."

This time the wizard's sly smile looked genuine. "Good. I'd like to leave here on good terms and with a nice 'fuck you' to the stiffs back on Earth."

***

Eyes. Ears. Ventura's got 'em all over the ship, and I don't mean the organic kind. We need to nip that in the bud before we get far with this job. This isn't the gallery security, just run-of-the-mill cheap-ass snooping. That doesn't mean it's a cakewalk ... no, that's not what a cakewalk means ... no, not that either ... it just means easy, ok? It won't be easy ... well, OK then, maybe it will. Well, Handkerchief, I'll defer to your expertise on this one. Do what you gotta, just blind those surveillance systems, but, you know, don't be obvious about it.

Buried deep in the guts of the *Convoy Queen*, the data center was cleaner than many parts of the ship but still grimy enough to give any core-educated data tech nervous spasms just touching the access panels.

Fooshri pried loose panel after panel with her lower hands while the upper set browsed an unrolled mat whose many pockets contained a variety of electronics tools, many of which were nearly identical. Those tiny differences and knowing when and which to use were the difference between an amateur, a professional, and a virtuoso.

She was a professional.

Geeree Advanced Technical University taught these techniques as part of their graduate program in Law Enforcement and Military Technology. Fooshri had finished her degree but never reported for her stint in Phabian Investigative Services. Instead, she'd converted to the Galactic Seekers of Peace for just long enough to qualify for a conscientious objector exception. It had meant serving three months as a volunteer for a colonial preacher, but in the end, she'd come away with a set of criminal credentials that was hard to equal.

Data cards slid in and out of the computer core, dangling by still-connected fiber cables. In short order, the laaku electronicist had pieced together the basic system architecture of the ship and bypassed the tampering safeguards.

When Fooshri's datapad hooked in, it was via one of six dongles she'd brought along; this one matched the manufacturer's factory testing and debug protocol.

There was much to do and medium time in which to do it.

First things first, she found the security camera archives and redirected them to a continuous re-write loop. Now, every five seconds, the *Convoy Queen* would overwrite its own footage of the ship's security. Then, she changed the file directory structure such that the cameras correctly believed that it was November 15th, 2541, while anyone accessing the database would have their query offset by minus seven days. All weekly routines would remain in place, but it would be last week's feed they'd be seeing.

This included live surveillance monitoring.

Fooshri sang under her breath as she worked. She had no singing voice, but alone it didn't bother anyone.

"*Make the work fill the time,*

"*So it happens you are done,*

"*Smart with micro-circuitry splicing but not with rhymes,*

"*This song in Kejathi was much more fun.*"

She improvised as she went, translating one of the mnemonic tunes from Basic Engineering Memorization and adjusting on the fly. If only Human had a single word for micro-circuitry splicing, it wouldn't have been so rough. So many Kejathi words lacked direct counterparts; it was a shame so few laaku still spoke it.

After a time, Fooshri's datapad burst into an array of tiny rectangular flatpic feeds.

She grinned.

Her data was real-time. She was the only one aboard with live views of the ship's interior corridors, various angles on the cavernous swap meet space, and the hangars. The bridge of the ship, Ventura's private quarters, and the art gallery weren't covered by the system.

Their plan didn't care about the bridge.

Ventura didn't have any devices invading his own privacy.

As for the gallery? That was on its own isolated system, inaccessible from Fooshri's location and not her problem.

Placing a finger to the comm piece in her ear, she reported in. "Handkerchief to Chaplain: I'm in. Many image. Much surveillance. Proceed."

Someone's going to have to keep an eye on Ventura. He's the wild card in all this. Once we get him pinned down, we're good. Until then, we watch and wait. Watching and waiting being lookout jobs, that's Maverick and Copernicus ... no, that's not your job ... that either ... no, just watch and report when he goes back to his quarters ... Look, if you don't like it, you can sit this one out back on the ship. I'm sure Copernicus can handle this solo ... yeah, that's more like it.

The catwalks that ran all over the swap meet were the domain of the ship's all-sitharn guard squad. That didn't mean no one else could make their way up and poke around. It just meant they had to do it while dodging patrols of reptiles that had their attention fixed downward. Still, it wasn't a great plan to linger.

The upper reaches of the swap meet were a spiderweb of structural supports, conduits for various gasses, fluids, and power sources, and—most importantly—access ladders.

Brad slouched in the elbow of a V-shaped steel support trellis. He straddled a device he'd magnetically attached to the beam, periodically checking through the lens to see if he had it lined up correctly.

"Little to the right."

Through the sight of the digital telescope, he watched the reflection in a distant mirror angle the wrong direction.

"The other right. My right. Not yours."

Brad's comm griped, "*Select a frame of reference. Many lefts. Only one right.*" Muted laaku laughter punctuated the joke.

"*Knock it off. Comms clear except business,*" Dad snapped. Man, he was being a hardass all of a sudden. Give a guy a little authority, and he forgets his comedic roots.

The mirror angled again.

"Little farther."

"*Quantity. How many degrees is a little?*"

Brad gritted his teeth. "I dunno. A couple."

The mirror moved slowly, constantly. Jomek wasn't

allowing nitpicking to stop him from trying a new approach. Soon, a door came into view.

"Stop! Right there. No. Back about... a degree," Brad guessed. It wasn't enough. "Another degree... Got it. This is Maverick. Mirrors are in place. Eyes on V-man's bedroom door."

It had taken five mirrors to bounce the view around corridors and through halls, but Brad couldn't blame a rich fucker like Ventura for not wanting to have his front door visible from the swap meet. To him, the division of labor had seemed obvious. More closely related to monkeys, Jomek had the natural advantage climbing around the upper reaches of the ship. Unfortunately, his laaku friend was the only one of the two likely to align the rest of the mirrors.

"Confirmed. Now let's just hope you knuckleheads staked out the right door."

Brad flipped the bird to the general direction where Dad was, somewhere in the rented room they'd commandeered for the heist.

He wasn't worried about Jomek picking the right room. Humans made stupid mistakes like that, not laaku. No, Brad's worry was more fundamental. He needed to take a piss, and pissing off the side of the support beam sounded like a great way to draw attention to himself.

Would Jomek make it up to relieve Brad before he had to relieve himself?

━━━

If we want free run of the ship's guts, we need the resident mechanics out of the way. Someone with a top-notch autopilot and comm spoofing rig would be doing us all a big favor if there could be an... incident somewhere out in the deep astral. Quick job. High pay. Enough to lure their whole crew. I'll word the distress call.

Abelforth yawned as he adjusted their course after a 2.8 AU astral drop. No one out here was going to complain about the irregular depth, and it was as low as the shuttle's star-drive could manage.

Time was money. While that was always true, today it was truer than usual.

A laaku trade ship, the *Rabo Nathlet,* was itching to dock and had lost their mechanic in the same accident that had knocked out their main engines.

Common wisdom would have had it that a laaku ship was *all* mechanics when you boiled away the job titles and egos. But Abelforth knew there was a whole class of the talking chimps that couldn't fathom the delicate workings of tech—or lacked the patience to wait.

"What's our ETA?" Pravesh asked, looming over Abelforth's shoulder.

A quick check gave the answer. "Two hours, fourteen minutes."

Blenda joined them, crowding the cockpit area. "Tight. You lads better be homing missiles as soon as we dock."

"We'll make it. From the description the captain gave, sounds like a fuel conduit. If there's no structural damage to the reactor—"

"If..." Pravesh echoed ominously.

Abelforth ignored the pessimist. "That should be an in-and-out under an hour."

"Two and a half hours back, only you'll miss your shift."

"I'll call in sick," Abelforth answered smoothly. "Seamus will cover for me. Ticonderoga's never gonna know they didn't have an engineering department for a few hours." He sucked a deep breath, savoring an aroma that filled the stale air. Raising his voice, he called back, "Hey, how those kielbasas coming?"

A shouted voice from the ship's kitchen answered immediately. "Couple of minutes. Set the auto and get back here. Bring your appetites."

What was the point of the four of them playing hookey if they couldn't enjoy some grilled delicacies along the way?

If Ventura had paid them better, maybe none of them would have taken a strange ship up on a shady offer of bonus pay. But with side work like this, they'd all find a way to afford jobs somewhere better.

Someday.

———

OK. This is one of the key points of the whole deal. We need Ventura to stay out of his gallery while we're in there. That means no working in the office next door, either. He's got to be completely occupied elsewhere. Gremlin, this is your department. Use your contacts. Find someone who can be bought by the hour and paid up front. We don't want anyone chasing us for petty terras during the getaway. Any questions? ... You sure? ... Well, great. We'll front you the terras. Get to it.

Two women, neither as young at heart as they appeared outwardly, loitered in a seedy bedroom, fully clothed. One perched on the edge of the bed with more skin exposed than covered and looked ready to explode out of her limited attire at the slightest hint. The other hid behind a trench coat, hood, gloves, and goggles, leaning against the door, lest there be any misunderstanding about where the other was supposed to be.

"You sure you don't want to... you know... *do* anything while we wait?" the prostitute who called herself Lilac asked. She had her hair, nails, and lips tinted pale purple, with color-change contact lenses to match. It was, best Neeta could tell, her gimmick. By all accounts, Ventura liked a deeper, more classically royal hue of purple, but it had been enough to make a shopping decision in the *Convoy Queen's* red-light district.

"Waiting is doing something," Neeta told her sternly. "Don't worry. You're still clocking, prossy."

Lilac shrugged bare shoulders. "Your terras."

"My employer's. Big diff. I got my instructs; you get yours when the time's right."

"I'll remember," Lilac promised. "I'm using the money for—"

Neeta shot up a gloved hand. "Don't wanna know. I don't wanna think of you as some teacher or doctor just makin' ends. You're a prossy; just act it."

"Yes, ma'am."

Neeta gritted her teeth at the word but allowed silence to settle in.

"What's in the bag?" Lilac asked after a few minutes of fidgeting on the foot of the bed.

What would it hurt? Neeta kicked it over to her. "Your costume."

"Costume?" Lilac brightened instantly. She had a perfect smile that her parents had probably paid good money for. So she wasn't working her way up from nothing; either she'd alienated her family, lost them, or they'd fallen on hard times. "Is it something fun? Can I look?"

With a sigh born of boredom, Neeta relented. "Fine. Just don't ruin anything."

A quick zip and some rustled fabric later, and Lilac stood admiring a bodiced purple dress of Renaissance styling. She held it up in front of her and twirled as if it were a dance partner. "How elegant. How classy. Should I try it on?"

"Not that classy. It's stretch fit. Snaps down the back. Grab the shoulders and yank down. Nude instantly."

Lilac swayed over, biting her lip. "Should we practice?"

Behind her goggles, Neeta rolled her eyes. "No. I don't want to chance it ripping. It wasn't that expensive. I'd treat it like a one-off."

"I really feel like you're not having fun. Do *you* want to try it on? You said it's a stretchy." Lilac held out the garment.

"No."

"But if we're careful—"

"No!"

Lilac sighed theatrically, then laid the garment across the bed and sat down beside it.

"Don't worry. You'll get your 'fun.'"

Lilac smirked. "Oh, I'll have something to do. It's rarely fun. Especially as a present. No imagination. You paid for 'anything goes,' but unless it's the client asking for that, there's no imagination."

"You better be *good* for what you're making."

"Oh. I am. He, she, or they will never know."

"It's a he."

Lilac made a face. "*Never* any imagination, then. But, I'm sure he'll have the time of his life. And there's always a chance *he's* good."

Neeta bit the inside of her cheek.

"No, huh?" Lilac probed. "You cringed a little. It's OK. I'm getting paid. Anything more is a bonus. It's just a nice little pick-me-up when—"

"Can you just stop being a goddamn *person*?" Neeta huffed a moment to catch her breath that had started coming quick. "Sorry. I just don't like being here."

"You live on the ship, don't you?" Lilac asked with a furrow of tinted eyebrows. "You must know the deal."

"I do. It's just... I'm not used to being the one paying to fuck up someone else's life."

Lilac got up and crossed the room slowly. "You're not hurting me. I'm numb by now. There are just certain thoughts not to think. I'm here by choice. It's a compromise I decided to make—"

"What did I tell you?"

Lilac ignored her. "Until 9:00 a.m. ship time, anything goes. Right? It's just the two of us, and I don't judge. Tell me what I can do to you. Anything." She whispered the latter as she placed her hands on the door to either side of Neeta's shoulders.

Neeta shrank back. A squawk in her comm earpiece saved the day.

"*Maverick reported in. Ventura just hit his quarters ahead of a room service delivery. We've got our window. You a go?*"

Neeta ducked free and tapped to activate send mode. "Yeah. Just a costume change, and the package is on the way."

"Such a pity. Another time, maybe? I don't do discounts, but I won't charge extra."

Neeta shoved the dress into Lilac's hands. "Just get changed. And memorize this script." She tossed a datapad onto the bed.

"Shouldn't we have done that earlier?"

"It's short."

Lilac switched clothes in no time and without a shred of modesty. Neeta whirled so as not to appear eager to gawk. When she peeked back, Ventura's gift was fully clothed—albeit in a tear-away costume and flimsy slippers—reading her introduction.

"Got it."

"Out loud," Neeta prompted. "And no cheating."

Lilac clasped her hand to her wrist behind her back, both

hiding the datapad and displaying her cleavage to best advantage. She held her chin high, smiled sweetly, and proclaimed, "I'm here as a gift from Mordecai The Brown. He believed that a Renaissance man such as yourself deserved the company of a Renaissance woman for... whatever you like."

Neeta opened the door. "C'mon, Mona Lisa. Time to be utterly captivating until morning."

<hr>

With most of the mechanics out of the way, it would be a real shame if something were to happen to the Convoy Queen's *life support systems. Especially if it were to be a widespread problem, hard to track down shorthanded. Cucumber, gonna need you to do some of your finest Cucumbing here ... what? I can't call it Oblecking. That would defeat the point of the code names ... no, if just anyone could Oblek, it wouldn't be Oblecking, it would be regular old, garden-variety sabotage.*

And to be clear, don't kill the blowers or filters. Last thing we need is a real panic. A chilly day in Swapmeetville is all we need.

Oblek peeked out from a maintenance door before exiting into a vacant corridor in the warehouse zone of the *Convoy Queen.* His knapsack didn't clank or jangle or rustle with the myriad tools packed up inside because he wasn't a rank amateur.

Thanks to his precaution, the pack could have contained anything: snacks, toiletries, a change of clothes, kids' toys, musical instruments... even mechanics' tools. But there was nothing illegal or even particularly suspicious about a licensed and certified starship mechanic toting around the implements of his profession.

Especially when no one had spotted him coming out of the maintenance crawlspaces.

Oblek plodded down the hallway, to all outside observance lost in the contemplation of a simple and miserable life. Along the way, he paused in front of a blower vent. Innocuous most of the time, they were the lungs of a starship—or at least the nose holes where its breath came out.

Lukewarm.

Still, it was better than the 35°C that the system was set for.

"No time to be impatient. Too much to do."

Oblek was also in too big a hurry to scamper or run. Moving with inappropriate haste was suspicious, and suspicion led to uncomfortable conversations—conversations that took longer than hustling saved.

Making his way generally toward the administrative portions of the ship, he checked each time he came across a vent.

Tepid.

Following a map in his head, he traced along the life support ducts as close as he could without delving back into the world of crawlspaces.

Cool.

Farther he wandered.

Chilly.

Keeping commentary inward, Oblek nodded with approval.

The deathly chill of the vacuum out in the Black Ocean.

That was it. That was the bone-chilling cold that would force action.

Continuing to navigate via a map that existed only in the tender flesh of his mind, Oblek altered his course and headed straight for Vendor Services.

Located at the forward starboard corner of the swap meet

itself, Vendor Services was a concierge largely dedicated to providing power and fluids to the booths and stalls where peddlers from across ARGO space hawked their wares. But they also doubled as a dead letter box for complaints of all sorts, staffed by dull-eared humans who could reply with the same words to any grievance.

When Oblek arrived, he found the desk unstaffed.

A screen facing the prospective line of bellyachers declared: **ALL REPRESENTATIVES UNAVAILABLE AT PRESENT.**

Oh, this was good. Better than expected.

With a quick check that no one seemed to be watching the area closely, Oblek hopped the counter.

On the far side, he found the ship's internal comm system. Finding the menu a pleasantly intuitive variant of the stock Neutral Ergonomic Consideration touch navigator, he quickly located the recipient he desired.

"Hello, bridge?"

"*Who is this?*" a stern voice demanded. Oblek suspected that his heavy Kejathi accent gave away his status as a non-crewman.

"I am the lessee of stall Miko-Miko-seven-four," he replied without hesitation. "My mercantile duties were taking a break from me, and the corridors wandered me."

"*This comm is for official ship's business. Please return to your designated area.*"

"The life support. Is that not business for the ship? It has the kaput."

"*What are you talking about?*"

"The air, it is freezy-peazy. Few degrees. Much un-temperature. Very not meeting Code 47.811b of ARGO spaceworthiness."

"*We'll look into it.*"

"Here is no one," Oblek explained, gesturing as if there were a video feed. "I am the alone in your No Help booth."

"*This isn't your concern.*"

"If your mind is changed, Miko-Miko-seven-four. I am there. Mechanic with license from Phabian. Much credentials. Many experience. Reasonable fees."

"*Bridge out.*" The comm ended abruptly.

Oblek hopped the counter in the other direction and headed back to his family's stall. There was already a crispness in the air that had him shrugging the collar of his jacket closer around his neck.

Good.

Now he just had to get back to stall MM-74 before the bridge sent someone to hire him.

Hadn't they heard? There was a labor shortage aboard the *Convoy Queen*.

A comm panel chimed.

Robert Ventura fumbled absently for it.

Out of reach.

Soft, firm fingers took hold of his wrist and guided the wandering hand back to the bare hip it had been gripping a moment before.

"I should... I should probably... they know not... bother me... unless it... it's important."

"Shh... Nothing's important right now..." a sultry voice cooed.

The comm signal repeated.

Ventura reached again. "I really... should..."

The rhythmic rocking and bouncing ceased, and a warm, pliable form pinned him flat to the bed. A pair of mischievous, twinkling eyes met his as their noses touched tip to tip. "Do you need another?" She brought a vivid blue pill into his limited field of view, curtained by the fall of her hair, and waggled it tantalizingly between thumb and forefinger.

Ventura hesitated. Not that he suspected poison. She'd been searched upon arrival and lacked anyplace subtle to conceal... well, anything. No, his temptress and tormentor had discovered the bottle in his nightstand, recognized them for what they were, and administered one immediately. They were his pills. All the rage in the naughty upper social circles of the core.

His problem was that he'd taken three already, and before that night, he'd never gone beyond two.

"I don't know..."

The comm chimed again. Its call was distant, insignificant.

"I do," she promised. "I'm an expert. You're going to sleep like a conquering god tonight, but not before I've wrung every last bit of you out. It would be such a... such a *shame* to quit now." She bit her lower lip.

What the hell? If his heart gave out, there were worse ways to die. He nodded once and let her push the pill past his lips. Then she practically rammed it down his throat with her tongue.

Core-tech pharma kicked in almost instantly as a deviously calibrated chemical shell dissolved in his stomach. Chemicals flooded his veins.

The rocking and bouncing resumed.

The comm panel gave up.

Now Ventura's biggest mistake was hiring sitharn as his guards. They're notoriously hard-nosed and intractable, almost impossible to bribe, and utterly unsympathetic to mammals. Great traits in a thug if you pay them right. But they also barely qualify as warm-blooded. The life support snafu's gonna get the crew up in arms, but it's going to make the sitharn lethargic as hell. Once they're in a stupid stupor, we swoop and scoop our loot.

Yes, I know it didn't quite rhyme.

No. I wasn't trying. I'm just a natural poet.

If you don't like the poetry, find some other heist, Peanut.

Seriously, fuck off, Lou. It's a long plan, and I don't want to spend the whole day arguing about my flow.

Maverick and Copernicus, you two watch the guards for signs that they're getting drowsy.

Yes. No shit, it's going to be cold up there ... I dunno. Deal with it.

Brad hunkered in his steel cradle, peeking occasionally at the rig spying on the door to Ventura's quarters. Nothing interesting had shown up on the display since Neeta's friend had delivered herself. Brad had tried not blinking afterward, hoping to keep the image in his eyeballs, but his efforts had been in vain.

Even though the guy was about to lose a bajillion terras worth of Old Earth artwork, Brad envied Ventura something fierce.

With nothing but a boring lookout job and a partner dedicated to keeping comm silence even sitting a meter away, Brad's imagination wandered.

His share would be worth millions of terras. Even though they'd screwed over him and Jomek with half-shares apiece, the haul was just going to be *that* huge. The odds of Dad letting him pocket all that was less than zero; Brad's next heist was going to be wrangling back his rightful cut—half what he and Dad pulled in combined.

That was fair.

And since Dad never was, it was up to Brad to fair it back out.

A necessary evil, figuring out how to Robin Hoodwink his dad, was a task for after they'd secured their riches.

How to *spend* his future earnings, however, was perfect daydream fodder.

Brad wanted his own starship. Credentials could be purchased—black market until he was old enough to have all his docs legitimately. With millions of terras, that sounded like the kind of thing he could pull off. His ship wouldn't be a clunker like the *Radio City*, either. It would have shields, guns, a star-drive that could drop him 6 or 7 AU deep—unless he could convince Mort to ditch the Ramsey family and fly with him. Then, the void was the limit.

And women.

There were still plenty of women out there who held a man's youth against him. Presumably, most of them mistook youth for inexperience; he could understand not wanting to get involved with a clumsy or awkward lover. With the kind of cash he could flash, he'd get the leeway he needed to prove just how misguided those prejudices could be.

He'd have to start carrying a blaster. Kid on his own out in the galaxy—with money—was going to have to prove he was no pushover. Something big, nasty, and obvious would ride on his hip. Maybe an Edgart 470 or a Skorpion A12. Then he'd keep another blaster or two tucked away in concealed holsters.

But that was just when he was out slumming the borderlands.

Brad would also fund his racing career. If he couldn't convince a team from Comet League, Silde Slims, or Earth Circuit to pick him up, he'd finance his own team. Maybe some people would wonder where he got the terras to afford the franchise fee. Good luck. Plenty of people got rich in the border colonies without a good data trail of how. It happened. Presumably, even legitimately sometimes. At some point, terras were just terras; once he started winning races, no one could question the legality of *those* credits.

Once he was a star racer getting broadcast on feeds across all ARGO space, women would be lining up for a chance to be with him.

He'd have to hire someone to screen applicants, there would be so many.

Oh, and he'd convince Jamie to ditch Earth Navy to come work with him. She'd need to brush the rust off her hull, but she'd be an ace racer just like him. And she could quit dating losers and find some dopey pretty-boy to settle down with. Or hire her own screener and just sample what the galaxy had to offer. Neither of them had to fuck up their lives like Mom and Dad by settling down with kids too young.

"I believe sleep fell on one of the guards," Jomek reported. He passed Brad a pair of binocs and pointed with a gloved lower hand.

Brad gave the eyepiece spacing a quick tug before peering through in the direction his friend indicated. Indeed, one of the sitharn security dopes sat slumped on the catwalk with his back against one of the supports for the railing, head bowed and blaster lying limp across his lap.

He scanned the rest of the swap meet, adjusting the zoom on the binocs as needed.

All throughout the ship, armed sitharn were growing sluggish and slow. It wouldn't be long before all of them needed a long nap—or torpor, whatever they called it.

Brad commed in to HQ.

"Maverick to Chaplain: the alligators in the sky are falling. Repeat, alligators are falling *out* of the sky."

"It is a bad code," Jomek insisted, thankfully not on the heist comm channel. "The dinuh suggests iguana are sitharn."

"It's just DNA. Don't try to pronounce it."

"*Roger that, Maverick. Report back when all the alligators are roadkill.*"

"Iguana," Jomek replied, this time to Dad over the comm. "We are confusion with alligators. Much lizard. Zero alligator."

"I'm on it," Brad replied, shooting Jomek a scowl that said, "Just shut up about it."

The pair watched from the ceiling of the swap meet, clutching chem hand-warmers and wishing for a campfire, as sitharn after sitharn fell asleep on the job.

———

Cucumber, you're a shoo-in to get hired. You've got the credentials. You're willing to work cheap but not suspiciously cheap. And most importantly, you'll be on their mind when they're looking for a quick solution.

Oblek chatted with a customer of the imaginative sort; the human imagined himself to be the sort who could afford the high-quality merchandise he inspected with no sense of understanding that he was not. Nevertheless, Oblek used the human as a prop for the illusion that he was, in fact, interested in selling salvaged electronics at the moment.

"As you can see, the thermal trigger is linked directly to the targeting circuit. It's an older architecture that puts the manufacturing date somewhere pre-2520. I can't imagine paying the price you're asking for twenty-year-old hardware."

Oblek nodded along. Not a single statement in the human's negotiation was true. What he mistook for a thermal trigger was a beta ray detector. And it connected to the processing array; the device did not even have a targeting circuit. It had no targeting function at all. Worst of all, before Fooshri had scoured off the manufacturer's information and serial ID, it had boasted of being made in 2538, just three years prior.

"You are astuteness. We complete, perhaps, the null transaction. Retain terras. I retain merchandise."

"Yeah. Whatever, pal," the human grumbled as he departed into the throng of useless shoppers.

The shop felt empty without Fooshri and Jomek around to help out. Even as a cover story, it didn't feel right not having them here. Worse, the absence left Oblek with his own thoughts as his sole companion. Oh, and he had so many thoughts.

His idle brain delineated the potential paths down which this plan could go wrong.

The security system could have been recently updated.

The sitharn security people might have emergency warming garments that would counteract the growing cold.

One or both of the pre-adult sentients might act their age.

Whoever was in charge of interim hiring might decide to employ someone besides Oblek.

The latter eventuality pressed most firmly on his cerebral cortex. This was to be his big part of the plan. He had to be involved, or the sabotage might be undone by honest and effective effort. The heist could not stand up against simple honesty and efficacy.

Ducking behind a shelf so stacked with hand scanners that it provided privacy, Oblek spoke softly into his comm. "Much time. Very minutes. Jobs are not having me. The wasted chrono is the backwards chrono."

Chuck's voice came back calm and soothing. *"Hey, Cuke. This is your rodeo. Ride it how you need. I wouldn't unplug the life support yet—bad analogy, sorry—I wouldn't butcher the ...*

no, that doesn't work either. Just, hey, if you think you need to short-circuit the job-getting part, you do you."

"Much understanding. Very decision. I go. Wish the cucumbers excellent outcome."

"Break a leg or three."

Oblek closed the comm, shaking his head. "Much words. Few meanings. So human." He understood the basics of the sentiment. Chuck meant well but invoked bothersome superstition, implying the laaku couldn't manage without paranormal intervention.

Grabbing his tools, Oblek paused only long enough to post a screen facing the pedestrian traffic.

SOON RETURNING. RESPECT MERCHANDISE.

He was likely to get robbed. His only solace came when he weighed the risk against the gains due from the proceeds of the heist.

Not five minutes after he left, a uniformed officer of the starship *Convoy Queen* arrived bearing a requisition for a mechanic. She lingered a few minutes, then commed back to the bridge.

"Not here. We can't wait around. Post an all-points hiring and filter anyone with a known criminal record. Best we're gonna do on short notice. Doubt we'll find anyone else with Phabian Mechanics' Guild certs, though."

Peanut... no idea how that gadget of yours works. Just dummy us up some convincing fake paintings.

Lou connected Hose 6 to Port 12. Why the ports and hoses couldn't share identical numbers escaped him. He kept referencing the technical specs for the Home Rembrandt brand Instant Masterpiece Maker, hoping that the befuddling instructions would suddenly make sense. If there were some key revelation awaiting him further down the lettered list of activities to perform, none arrived.

"Tighten Hose 6 to per Unified Engineering Code A191, subsection 22." It required cross-referencing a document Lou didn't have access to, given the tight controls on omni connection within Ventura Convoy. Had he known in advance, he might have suggested the crew add tapping into an illicit data connection as part of their larger plans. "Why couldn't they just *put* the torque value in their instructions?"

Unfortunately, if this job never cleared escape velocity, Lou hadn't wanted to get shafted the cost of the auto-painting equipment. Taking it out of the manufacturer's packaging and assembling it instantly lowered its resale value.

He gave the hose fitting a snug twist with a wrench and called that good enough.

"Next, check Hose 6 for kinks or blockages."

Lou picked up the assembly and stared at it incredulously.

"Why couldn't you have told me that *before* I connected it? I could have just blown through it or stuck a rod down the length of—" He caught that he was talking to himself, or at least to an inanimate set of assembly instructions that couldn't possibly be listening.

"*Yo, Peanut. How's it coming?*" barked Lou's comm earpiece, startling him to the point where he dropped the datapad with his instructions.

Lou swore several times before opening his comm to reply. "Be coming along quicker if you didn't keep nagging. Second painting is drying now. I'm about to load up the third. And for Chrissake, keep off my case. This is delicate work."

"*Thought some robot was supposed to be painting.*"

"I *could* wait with the finished masterpieces in the machine until everything dried. Or we could speed things up, and I quickly withdraw the wet works wight a way." Lou grimaced. "Right away."

"*Well, make it snappy. We got sitharn getting drowsy out there. Almost time to move.*"

"Yeah, yeah," Lou snapped. He cut the comm.

It took another twenty minutes before he finished assembly, and another ten to run through the initial setup routine. By the time he'd loaded the primary color cartridges, the plasticanvas, and the file to be copied, he knew he was in trouble.

As van Gogh's Wheatfield with Crows emerged from a rapid-fire series of flicks and stabs from a brush-looking stylus wielded by the Instant Masterpiece Maker, he looked up options in the settings menu.

It had slower speed, but the default was the fastest it went.

"Shit," he muttered to himself.

The instructions insisted he allow two to three hours for proper drying, depending on local atmospheric humidity. *Rex Piscis*, being a starship, was as arid as you'd expect. No one wanted mold or that icky clamminess that came with dank air. No one human, at least. But even the two-hour low end was going to burst blood vessels in Chuck's eyeballs if Lou came back to him with that kind of delay.

So, as Degas's The Dance Class began printing, Lou took Annie's fingernail anhydrater and painstakingly helped the drying along. In the process, he smudged the lower edge of Wheatfield with Crows, right across the walking path.

"Shit, shit, SHIT..."

He smoothed out the fingerprint as best he could. Enough that he wouldn't damn himself with P-tech physical evidence. But there was no overlooking that he had fucked up.

Shaking his head, he went back to drying. "No helping it. Gonna get covered up by the frame, anyway."

▭

Once we've got the ship's security force sleepy—and let's be fair, maybe a few cases of hypothermia and frostbite in the med bay— it's time to make our move. Ishmael, this is your time to shine. And you'd better shine like Sol, otherwise we're all gonna be standing here with our keys in a fishbowl and not a spouse to be found.

"Door's clear," came a child's voice over the comm. Ramsey's boy. Not a bright spot on the comedian's criminal resume.

Joe had to trust that this was good enough. After all, even a teenager could tell the difference between a hallway with people in it and one that was empty.

His shadows were the shiprat and the laaku woman. The former was clearly just a babysitter unless she'd held out during the crew's inventory of relevant skills. Pickpocket. Gossip. Scavenger. Hustler. She was the sort of low-level operative Joe would have *preferred* on lookout duty over Oliver Twist and the Artful Dodger up in the rafters.

"If don't. I will," Handkerchief stated bluntly. She'd heard the same comm. If Joe didn't crack the security lock on this door, he had little doubt she'd bypass the system through less inconspicuous means.

"I got this," Joe assured her. He held his datapad to the hand scanner, screen first. The device blinked through a series of test codes, none resembling a hand scan in any sense. But the system needed factory debugging, and the flash sequence had been deemed a better option than baking employee handprints into the software.

Clunk.

Whoosh.

The door slid open. Joe pinwheeled a hand to usher

everyone through in haste. His two companions didn't need to be told once, let alone twice. In seconds, Joe keyed the door to snap closed behind them.

"We're in," Gremlin reported into her earpiece.

"Copy that. No one spotted you."

Joe paused for a breath to survey the gallery. A senator's ransom of precious Earth artwork stared serenely back at him.

Gremlin shook her head. "The shit Solars pay for. I've stolen old datapads that take better pics'n this."

"Money is in the eye of the bag holder," Handkerchief quoted errantly. She unslung her backpack and headed for Magritte's The Son of Man.

Joe got to work immediately.

Ventura had done a nice job with his setup. None of the security panels were casually visible in the perusal of the gallery. But with a hand scanner and an insider's knowledge of the power signature of the closed alarm system, he traced the owner's console in seconds.

Gremlin grunted as she dragged a plush love seat across the room.

Joe glanced up. A chivalrous impulse to lend a hand distracted him only for a breath before he returned to the task at hand.

"Please don't have updated to the latest patch..." he repeated under his breath, over and over.

Over and over.

Sweat beaded on Joe's forehead as the system processed his request for superuser access.

Handkerchief snapped flatpics, documenting the layout of the room.

Gremlin finished rearranging the furniture and collapsed onto the chair she'd just moved, huffing for breath.

Joe continued his mantra past the point where the system ought to have either spat back an error or let him in.

Had Ventura made custom updates? A silent alarm that wasn't in the installer specs for this setup?

Or had it really not been as long as it felt?

Joe hadn't set a timer or checked a chrono before getting started. With Ramsey running the show, they weren't exactly working to a stopwatch.

Bwink!

The panel turned green.

"I'm in!"

Fingers flying, Joe deactivated display after display. As the ambient lighting went out, so did the magnetic locks for the display cases and the alarms that would go off had anyone tried to force them.

"It's a five-minute reboot cycle. Work quick."

Work quickly they did. One a burglar by trade and the other possessed of laaku dexterity, they extracted the paintings in no time at all.

Joe put a finger to his ear, pressing the key to open his comm. "We're ready. Where's our ride?"

The comm panel of the *Radio City* pinged.

Becky stared past the paused holovid, eyes failing to focus on the frozen image of two anthropomorphic bears playing in a Wax-i-Rod-green forest. From the floor, the sound of dolls flying—evident by the mouth sounds of children making "twinkle" noises—told her that both Rhi and Mikey were present and accounted for.

Becky was sober.

The comm pinged again.

It was just another offer. She didn't need to answer it.

The comm pinged again.

They'd give up sooner or later. The *Radio City* wasn't going anywhere while the hobbyist criminals were amok.

One of the doll noises ceased.

Footsteps.

"Hullo?" Mikey asked, voice coming from the cockpit. "Wow. That sounds like a lot of money. No, my daddy can't come to the comm right now. May I take a message?"

Fuck.

With a grunt of effort more mental than physical, Becky pried herself from the living room couch.

"Baby, how many times I gotta tell you? Don't go answering the comm."

She picked her way through a minefield of toys ranging from building blocks to toddler board games. The clutter had multiplied like little plastic rabbits all over the floor. Maybe the next game could be The Cleanup Race. Despite her best efforts to throw the game, Becky was the reigning and undefeated champion.

"But, Mom—" Mikey began, leaning forward to support himself on the copilot's chair and reach the comm panel. When had he gotten big enough that he could reach without standing on the seat?

"Butts are for sitting."

Mikey scowled. "The other kind of but." He pointed to the comm panel. "They're offering us a lot of money for our spot here. Should we take it?"

Reaching past her son, Becky opened a channel. "Yo, this ain't up for sale. Go beg a berth from someone else." She killed the connection and turned to Mikey. "Y'all gonna go back and play with your sister till dinner. Catch my drift?"

Mikey puffed his cheeks in a melodramatic sigh. "Copacetic."

Becky smirked at his use of the word. Trying to sound grown-up when he was anything but. Clearly, he was getting bored. Feeling particularly Mom at the moment, Becky felt the inspiration sneak up on her.

"Ya know what?"

"What?" Mikey asked dutifully.

"We're gonna craft."

A pair of disbelieving eyes beamed up into hers. "REALLY?"

"Go in the cargo hold and find the box. I got some stuff you two can play with."

Mikey didn't need to be told twice. He practically left an ion trail as he blasted off in search of the Box of Wonders. Containing scissors, glue, cotton balls, glitter, and various implements of adding color to different surfaces, it was the messiest activity allowed aboard the *Radio City*—and that included Mikey's attempts at cooking.

Meanwhile, Becky retrieved a stack of pamphlets she'd collected during the family's tour of the swap meet. Comparatively few of the vendors passed out plastisheet adverts touting their capitalist offerings. But the damn place was big enough that they added up.

By the time Becky had accumulated the adverts and filtered out a few that featured adults-only products, Mikey was already at the kitchen table unloading his tools like a racing circuit mechanic. Rhi had joined and was deviously commandeering anything that glittered.

Becky plunked down the stack of plastisheets. "What do we wanna make today?"

Mikey scanned the pamphlets while Rhi took one

seemingly at random and attacked it with a pair of kiddie scissors.

"Let's make a parade!"

Becky nodded along. "Groovy."

Though she knew the mess they were making, Becky got into the flow of the game. At Mikey's direction, she worked on marching band costumes. An assortment of mismatched advert models acquired pink-dyed cotton-ball hats. Mikey drew musical instruments with a marker and traced them with scissors. Rhi made confetti. Even with safety scissors, Becky winced watching her chop and hack with reckless abandon.

It wasn't fun. It wasn't mind-blowing. But hanging out with the littles gave Becky a sort of deep satisfaction that was hard to describe.

She loved the little buggers. If only they weren't so damned *needy*.

Becky consoled herself when she realized it could be *her* out there risking her neck to keep the food coming in and the fuel rods burning. There wasn't money enough in the galaxy for her to swap places with Chuck.

━━━

Chuck Ramsey tipped his chair back and took a long swig of Mars-brewed ale. The guy selling it was full of shit about the brew's origins, but it was better than 90 percent of the swill he downed in the name of frugality. Platters of cheeze-with-a-Z nachos and factory-stamped chicken wings lay devastated before him. Propping his feet on the empty chair beside him, Chuck tried to imagine this was what it would be like as CEO of a major corporation.

Upgrade the food.

Switch from beer to fancy liquor.

Instead of a spare conference room chair, it would be a lackey acting as a footstool.

He could get used to this.

"Chaplain, still waiting on that rover."

Joe was one exhausting sonovabitch. Heists didn't award bonus points for finishing ahead of schedule.

Chuck took his channel selector and filtered it to only include Lou and Oblek. "Peanut, how's it coming with those postcards?"

"Inbound to Cucumber. Hold your horses."

Fiddling with the selector again, he raised Brad and Jomek. "Yo, Maverick and Copernicus. Things are coming together. How we looking for extraction?"

"Door's clear. It's a door. He's the boss. And he's got his boink on. Can't imagine anyone's allowed to bother him."

Chuck gritted his teeth. *This* was precisely why his instincts told him not to involve the kid. The lure of an extra half share for minimal risk had proved too tempting to pass up, and now he was paying the price. "Watching the door doesn't mean staring at it. It means watching vantages that can *see* the door, making sure anyone coming and going doesn't notice the crew exiting."

"Wait. I thought we were keeping tabs on the boss."

"Both. It's both, Maverick. Can't you keep an eye on both? It's not like they're on opposite sides of the ship."

"Duh. Of course not. I could switch back and forth, but—"

"There's two of you. For fuck's sake, there's two of you. You each need to watch one."

"Who gets which?"

"I don't *care* who takes which."

"Caring about details is your job. You've got the flight stick of this heist-mobile. Maneuver us."

"Hang tight," Chuck snapped before switching channels to

the gallery team. "Gremlin, I need to pull you for lookout duty."

"*Got two lookies already. Stow it. I'm surfing a couch waiting for our fakies.*"

"Delegate."

"*Ishmael's gonna break his neck tryna balance up here. And four hands don't come with arms long enough to reach.*"

Fuck. She was right. Not that he had a great read on Joe's physicality, but he didn't seem like the nimble sort. Not like Neeta. She was nimbleness incarnate. Just being in her presence, Chuck had to check his pockets out of paranoia.

He considered shooing Brad and Jomek out of their sky perch. Putting them on the ground. But that meant exposing them to risks he wasn't willing to justify to Becky. And it was one thing explaining away a narrow escape. It was another bringing up the subject of bail, criminal records, and prison sentences. Because if there was one thing Brad wasn't, it was careful.

"Fine. Proceed as planned. I'll think of something." Chuck closed the comm.

Open-mouthed noshing from the far end of the table drew Chuck's eye. Mort was snarfing down chicken wings like he didn't know what was in them and drinking beer straight from the catering pitcher.

The wizard glanced up from the platter he'd taken all to himself. "Don't look at me when you promise you'll think of something. I only got half a conversation, and that was enough to know you've pickled yourself into a jar here."

"We've lost confidence that our exit path is clear."

Mort sighed and wiped his mouth with the cuff of his suit. "Lemme guess. Your solution is..." He wiggled his fingers like they were a hieroglyph that finished that sentence.

"No, I—" Chuck caught himself. Why overthink this? Mort

hadn't *sunk* the *Nazareth*. Sure, it had taken Earth Navy-trained engineers days to sort the place back out, and it was built like a brick shithouse compared to the *Convoy Queen*, which was a corrugated aluminum latrine at best. But the only ones killed by Mort's magic had been intentional victims. The weary resignation in those wise, planet-crushing eyes warned him off pressing launch on the escape pods too quickly. "Well, OK. Maybe I considered it. But, no. You just need to take a walk around the halls where our team is working and shoo people away."

"With magic."

"With *whatever*. I don't care. Be disgusting. Be belligerent. Impersonate a security goon. Set up a safety cordon. Be creative."

"Sounds like a two-person job."

Chuck opened his mouth to snap off a quick reply, but his quick-replier wasn't loaded with a comeback to that one. The process of reloading made him look briefly like an aquarium fish. "No. I'm coordinating this whole shebang."

Mort pushed back his chair and stood, using a disposable towel to clean his fingers one by one. "Well, from the sound of it, you're not doing such a shebang-up job of it. I didn't let you rope me into some high-school theater production of a crime. We don't even need to dirty our hands here. At worst, we're signing up for sore feet."

Chuck deflated. Reaching into his pocket, his hand closed around a small electronic device. He placed it on the conference table and gave it a shove, shuffleboarding it down to Mort's end.

"What's this? One of those earwigs you talk to?"

"Yup. Jam it in your ear, and don't fuck with its science."

"I don't let scientists tell me what to do; no way in hell I'm obeying the electric demons they trap in plastic."

Chuck squeezed shut his eyes. "C'mon. Just put it in and listen. You'll hear what's going on with everyone else. I'm not enough of a chump to think I can *order* you to do much of anything."

━━━

Going mobile. Stick to the timetable—what's left of it—and don't bother me unless it's urgent.

"Great," Lou said, tilting his head back as if the steel ceiling could offer solace. "Now we're *headless* chickens."

"Landfowl are unimportant. Motion is key," Oblek called down quietly from the ventilation duct above. Maneuvering the vent cover back through the hole it was meant to regulate had been no easy trick. Space in the light-gauge rectangular duct was scarce. Gripping the cover by the louvres required strong, thin fingers—which luckily the laaku had. With help from below, the task would have been simple. Yet relying on Lou did not seem wise just then.

Oblek motioned for Lou to pass the bundle to him. The human obliged, stretching arms to their limit as the mechanic did likewise.

Illegal copy-paintings changed hands.

Oblek painstakingly reversed his removal of the vent cover.

"You need a hand with that?" Lou offered.

"Plenty hands. Much concentration. Quiet appreciates you."

Oblek levered the louvre into place and vanished from his friend's view.

"I don't like this. Plan gets a little sketchy from here..."

In the privacy of the conduit, Oblek rolled his eyes. Yes. It was a plan of well-modulated stupidity. Yet their victim was human. And arrogant. And rich enough that Oblek didn't feel the least bit sorry for robbing him. Focusing on the wrongness of navigating a life-support conduit did not help the plan advance.

"Hide. Ceilings are suspicious companions. Very walking. Much absence."

"Good luck," Lou replied with a curt nod.

Oblek held his word. He waited until Lou was gone.

"Asshole," the laaku declared. How dare the human sentence him to relying on luck. This was a skill endeavor. Luck was for the unskilled, the unprepared, the unworthy. Basically, for humans.

Doing his best to concentrate on the task at hand, Oblek turned his attention to the toy rover that Jomek had not played with in five years, eight months, and a number of days Oblek was chagrined to realize he could not recall exactly. "Aging is the curse of the successful," he muttered to himself in Kejathi.

The rover operated on a short-range datapad link, boosted by an auxiliary antenna Oblek had added for the occasion. It had a towing capacity of 12 kg on an untreated stainless-steel surface, far exceeding the load of the forged paintings supplied by Lou.

Hooking the strap of Lou's pack directly to the welded-on tow hitch would have worked for a certain geometry of ductwork. However, the *Convoy Queen* did not use 45-degree turns or a smooth-curve system. Hard right angles the whole way meant that Oblek had to allow his payload to drag half a meter behind so the rover and pack had room to articulate.

He had made all the necessary calculations and pre-cut a length of cable to size.

In no time, Oblek powered up the rover and sent it off on its journey to Ventura's gallery.

The initial draft of the plan had called for the laaku to act in place of the rover. However, though smaller than most adult humans, he was not a snake. The ducts narrowed to the point where Oblek would have required pneumatic pressure built behind him to extrude him through the final sections of ducting.

Jomek's rover allowed him to survive the painting transfer.

With a whirr and a grumble, the rover set off.

Oblek monitored the vehicle's journey from his datapad. The hastily constructed interface overlaid a three-dimensional model of the ship's life support system. Without a camera aboard, Oblek's program counted revolutions of the rover's wheels to track its progress, including the mismatched rotations of the skid-steer turning method during turns.

Pre-programmed and on passive monitoring, Oblek reclined against the walls of the cramped conduit and reported in.

"Cucumber here. Fakie-paints going there. Gallery will arrive with deliveries in eight minutes, eleven seconds from... now."

"*Copy that. We'll be ready for 'em,*" Joe replied.

As the sound of the rover faded to distant echoes, Oblek perked his ears and listened for signs of anyone *inside* the ship's guts who might be looking for the source of the ice-cold air or investigating why the air flow to the gallery had cut off entirely.

Oblek was no fool. He'd welded this duct shut upwind of his position. Otherwise, he'd have been a laaku-pop by now.

━━━

Meanwhile, an hour outside Ventura Convoy...

Captain D'Artagnan Richter drummed his fingers on the arm of his command chair.

This was always the boring part of a pirate's life.

At the comms, Belisarius pulled his headset away from one

ear, scratched his stubble, and chewed the inside of his cheek a moment before reporting. "Cap'n. Yer not gonna like this; just getting out there afore you come on a sudden bout of heartburn."

"Go ahead," Richter grumbled. "Bad news never got sweeter with ripening. Just rots and stinks all the worse."

Belisarius cleared his throat. "Well, then. That was ops at the *Convoy Queen*. Seems they's got a bit of a backlog. Not a single Class A berth open."

Busy season, it seemed. Richter sighed. "What's the wait?"

"They're just guessin', you see. Ain't like it's a fixed orbit."

"Spit it out!"

"Midmorning tomorrow... optimistically."

"Get us prio one. Fuck these unsheared sheep. Who they think they're dealing with?"

Looming at his right hand, his second in command, Delvin, leaned in close. "You advised me to warn you about gaffes."

"Yeah?" Richter replied quietly, frowning.

"Your implications about farm animals and what ought to be done with them."

Richter's eyes widened. Shit. "Thanks," he mumbled. Raising his voice, he addressed his bridge crew. "Open me a channel to the *Convoy Queen*."

Belisarius held up an index finger, then chopped it down toward his captain.

Richter stood. "This is D'Artagnan P. Richter, captain of the *Quasar Cannibal*. My men are weary, and my cargo hold is full. I expect an empty berth waiting for us when we arrive, or we're boarding you by force. Understood? And in case you didn't, let me make it clear as shit for ya. I want terras for my haul. I want workers to unload it. I want space to sell it. Or I want some rich fucker to buy it wholesale. Don't matter. But like hell am I waiting sixteen hours for you stim-addled coin salesmen to mosey out of the way."

He hand-signaled back to Belisarius, and the comms officer confirmed he was no longer being broadcast.

Richter slumped into his chair, knowing he'd have a spot ready and waiting when he arrived.

Delvin leaned down and quietly informed him that, "Sir, shit isn't clear."

Chuck paced with his hands in his pockets, trying to make it look like he was waiting for someone. The outskirts of the swap meet tended to spill over into the surrounding hallways, but casually so. Smokers smoking, stim users injecting, lovers negotiating payment terms; no one lingered long. Business was for quieter locales. Deals concentrated closer to the hangars or within the meet itself.

He half considered the purchase of a cigar just to look less conspicuous.

Mort, on the other hand, threw himself into the role.

When a mixed pair of tesuds meandered in the direction of the way to Ventura's gallery, the wizard swooped in. "Have you considered devoting your soul's endeavors to the words of Baphomet? Immortal service to the Astral Light in exchange for all the galactic pleasures you can—no? Are you sure? Well, what about a donation to help the more enlightened? You can pay hardcoin or enter into a bonded service contract..."

The only thing keeping the pair from turning tail and running was thick-blooded tesud physiology. As soon as the torpid bipeds could reverse course—and the chill in the air that no number of impromptu open fires in the swap meet could combat—they vamoosed.

Chuck shot the mad preacher a wink. "Where'd you get that mumbo jumbo?"

"Fucker out of Kingston ran off to the nethers of the galaxy to start a Baphomet cult. Fella had some good points, too. Half considered joining, but the food was shit."

"What happened to him?"

Mort smirked. "About what you'd expect."

Comedic instincts suggested an emperor's-new-clothes gag that Mort laid bare. The poet in his soul would have allowed karma to have his followers turned against him by his own teachings. But Chuck had known Mort long enough to suspect the obvious: that there was likely little more left of the self-appointed prophet than ash and a scribbled-out name in a library ledger.

A herd of foot traffic, jostling for position, came not to interfere with Chuck and Mort's vigil but to bypass it on the way to some common destination elsewhere.

Mort leaned against a wall, watching impassively. Chuck couldn't help his curiosity; he pulled aside a pedestrian who wandered within arm's reach.

"Where's everyone going?"

"Pirate haul comin'. Act quick, maybe you can hire on." The guy looked Chuck up and down. "Maybe not. You don't look like you need the terras."

"Pirate haul?" Mort echoed once Chuck let his personal newsreader go on his way.

"Ehh. No big deal. Brad pitched it before we decided on this venture. Easy money."

"Pirates pay well for grunt labor?"

It was Chuck's turn to smirk. "No. They keep lousy track of their inventory. These idiots rob them half-blind, while the pirates just think it's bait for their next attack. Some of the shit coming aboard's just gonna get plundered again from its new owners, legit or not."

Mort harrumphed. "Economics..."

"It's all good. We just need to keep up the pace of things. This chaos will be great cover for our exit."

"How's that going, anyway?"

Chuck pressed a finger to his ear, making his comm easier to hear. "Dunno. 'Bout time to check in."

<hr>

Neeta stood with both feet atop the cushioned back of the love seat in Robert Ventura's gallery. Originally, it provided a cozy view of half a billion terras worth of stolen artwork. Now, it had a sidewalk view of her boots. Toes flexed and soles wobbled as she maintained her precarious perch.

Perhaps she could have waited at ground level. That had been a judgment call born of optimism. Now, she was stranded with her pride on the line. Hopping back down would look amateurish, rather than foisting that moniker onto the laaku toy pilot who was overdue in delivering their forgeries.

Joe knelt on the floor with Fooshri watching over him as he laid out the artwork one piece at a time.

The hiss of a can sprayer set Neeta's teeth on edge. "You sure that stuff's safe?"

"Yeah," came the curt reply.

"I don't wanna try fencing running oil paint to a—"

"It's the same stuff fancy galleries use to handle priceless masterpieces," Joe snapped as he swept the spray back and forth, back and forth, making his way methodically down the entire surface of Raphael's Saint George and the Dragon.

"As long as no drippy dragons," Fooshri replied. "Blaster makes drippy wound, not spear."

"You're not helping," Joe remarked without looking up from his task.

Another sound caught Neeta's ear just then. Beneath the hiss of spraying, the whir of an electric motor.

"It's coming!" she announced.

"Much quiet. Little voices," Fooshri scolded her.

Neeta raised both middle fingers in a gesture that she hoped translated better than words to the English-deficient laaku.

"That stuff gonna dry in time?" Neeta asked urgently. They'd gone from being the ones waiting to the ones potentially holding up the whole operation.

"It doesn't dry. It forms a flexible protective barrier that will break down and evaporate in approximately three to four hours. We can use these paintings as place mats at the greasiest barbecue joint in St. Louis Prime, and they'll be fine. We can cover our heads with them in a rainstorm. At no point in the process does it 'dry.'"

The comm in Neeta's ear blared suddenly. *"Hey, keep the channel clear. We're not here for a science lesson. Especially a certain one of us who's about ready to stomp on his comm."*

"Roger that, Chaplain," Joe replied without a hint of remorse. He tapped his ear twice.

Neeta looked up at the vent. "Hey. The whirring stopped." She engaged her own comm. "Cucumber, this is Gremlin. Grab coffee on your own time."

There was no reply.

"Cucumber, you read me?" Neeta waited a moment, then added, "Hey, *asshole*. You're bogging the game here."

Fooshri entered the channel. "Dilator of my loins, are you endangered?"

Neeta cringed, hoping it didn't show that she understood conversational Kejathi.

"My rivet-gun of love, you begin to worry me..."

"*Many apologies. Much contrition,*" Oblek replied a moment later. "*My position stumbled onto fools who were hired for the fixing job that did not obtain me. Await the await-ables. Your position will arrive in less than ninety-four seconds.*"

The whir in the air ducts resumed.

Neeta breathed a sigh of relief.

On the floor, Joe and Fooshri rolled up a life's fortune in ancient canvases like nothing more than temporary promotional signage. From her high vantage, Neeta took one quick, final inventory before the bland backs of the masterpieces were all that was left visible. The names and artists came right off the placards Ventura had installed beneath the exhibits—they could have sent anyone literate with a memory better than a goldfish and not bothered involving a wizard in this job.

She took stock as they became unidentifiable rolled-up tubes.

Wheatfield with Crows, by Vincent van Gogh.

The Dance Class, by Edgar Degas.

The Son of Man, by René Magritte.

Saint George and the Dragon, by Raffaello Sanzio da Urbino, a.k.a. Raphael.

Lastly, there was Orange Prince, by Andy Warhol.

None of them was anything Neeta had heard of before this business, but the five images would be etched in her mind for the rest of her life.

The whirring stopped again.

Neeta peered through the open hole in the vent.

Nothing.

Neeta was back on the comm in an instant. "Hey. What's the deal? You compro again or something? My beater can't take these hiccups. Ya know?"

The motorized noise had been getting louder and louder. The toy rover had to be close.

"*Small math. Few revising. Unexpected stop at corner. Solution imminent.*"

Neeta gritted her teeth.

Chuck came over the heist channel. "*Yo, fuzz-man. Thought math was a species specialty.*"

Fooshri jumped to her husband's defense. "His badness of math is not typical of engineers. He muchly tries." Well, at least that sort of counted as a defense.

The whirring resumed in a short series of fits and spurts before the sound grew louder and continued advancing toward the gallery vent.

"*You smell!*" Oblek declared triumphantly.

"Huh?" Neeta replied with her comm still open.

Seconds later, Chuck came on. "*Our esteemed linguistics expert thinks he might have meant 'Eureka.'*"

"Yes," Oblek replied cheerily. "*Much odor. Many success. Victorious fakeness is proximate.*"

The plastic grumble from the motorized rover grew. By the time it arrived, Neeta worried just how noisy the device truly was. When it appeared at the edge of the vent covering, it stopped.

"*The front, are two centimeters between the opening?*" Oblek asked.

"Close enough," Neeta declared. Reaching overhead, she grabbed the toy and rotated it until she hooked a gloved finger on the length of cable tethering their forgeries.

"*Good-good. Worry had me. Much theory. Many guesswork. I leak from joy.*"

Seated on the floor as Joe finished gathering the artwork, Fooshri made yak-yak-yak gestures with three hands and rolled her eyes. "Yes, dear. Shut up about how smart you are."

Behind her goggles, Neeta blinked. "When'd your English polish up?" The laaku had spoken with only the faintest of Kejathi accents.

"Oblek is traditional. He doesn't like when Jomek and I make him sound traditional. Very paradox. Much dumbass. He plays it up when trying to sell something. He can speak almost good English if he tries."

"Should I be insulted?" Joe asked lightheartedly as he passed the bundle of art up to Neeta in exchange for the fresh-printed phonies.

"Yes," Fooshri replied with a grin. Everyone seemed happier now that the sketchy part of the plan had gone off with only minor glitches.

Neeta stuffed the paintings into the knapsack tied to the back of the rover. "Loaded up. Toy need a push to start her up?"

"Place vent hole on edge of back wheels."

Neeta followed the instructions, juggling the knapsack in one hand while she maneuvered the rover into position with the other. The cable was too short to set it down and still have the rover in the ductwork. "Done. Now what?"

The rover lurched forward. *"Push-push. Close up behind. Much trust. Very competence. Thank you."*

With the slack in the cable rapidly vanishing into the duct, Neeta hastily shoved the knapsack up behind it. As the rover towed their loot out of view, Neeta saw her hopes for the future going with it.

It was a trifling task to replace the cover, yet Neeta just lingered, staring, listening to the fading sounds of the rover.

"Yo, you going spectator on us?" Joe demanded. He and Fooshri were already working to install the paintings back in their appropriate display cases, referencing the flatpics Joe had taken earlier.

Remembering her duties, Neeta popped the vent cover back into place. And secured it. She hopped onto the comm. "Gremlin to HQ. Bon voyage."

"*Super duper,*" Chuck came back instantly. "*Look, Gremlin. Ishmael and Hankie can handle the tidying. I need you up in the lookout nest.*"

"*Three* lookouts?" she scoffed. "As if."

"*No. Making sure we have at least one. It's getting chaotic on Saint Lootings Days out here, and I want eyes up there who know this place well enough to know what wrong looks like.*"

With a sigh, Neeta conceded his point. "Fine. On my way."

The door slid shut behind Neeta.

Joe glanced at his datapad, still hooked into Ventura's system. Still blind. Still safe. Still going according to plan.

"Hurry it up over there," he called out to his lone compatriot without actually checking on her progress.

"Show flatpic. Which side is up?" Fooshri answered.

Joe opened his mouth to chew her out, then saw that she'd hung The Son of Man and Orange Prince already—both properly oriented—and was starting on Wheatfield with Crows. "Don't kid around. This is serious."

"Less pooka pooka with the lips. More flicka flicka with the fingers."

Biting back a retort, Joe set back to work on installing Saint George and the Dragon exactly as they'd found it. He cross-checked his reference image regularly, making sure the work was aligned properly in its frame. Some art collectors were true connoisseurs, experts in their own right, even if they had no respect for the wider art community or the general public.

Ventura struck Joe as the other sort. He just couldn't risk

that the miser's trophy case was more than a mere scoreboard for his wealth. The key to this getaway was the idea that no one even suspected a theft. In Joe's ideal scenario, Ventura wouldn't find out until he tried to sell one and had an appraiser take a closer look.

Just as soon as Joe finished locking the case over The Dance Class—with Fooshri looking on impatiently—he got a notification on his datapad. It was from the alarm system.

SYSTEM RE-ARMED.

"What?" he asked the screen. Why had the alarm reactivated? Locking when the exhibits were all closed would have been an option at installation, but he and the other installers had always advised against the setting due to the number of false positives. It was basically viewed by the on-site teams as a known bug, despite the software guys insisting it had been requested by clients and had to be included.

But Joe had been here. He'd worked on the gallery security loop. He hadn't turned that setting on.

Fooshri peered over his shoulder. "Your fix has slipped. Please remedy. Quickly."

"Right," Joe muttered, fingers already moving across the screen. "This shouldn't have happened."

The laaku nodded. "Yes. Many things have should-nots. Paintings should not have been stolen. Us should not stand here—"

"No. I mean, Ventura must have hired an outside consultant to tweak the system. Like he knew Iron Moon might pull an inside job someday. Paranoid bastard."

The laaku gestured frantically toward his datapad. "Less pooka pooka with lips. More tappa tappa on screen."

"Yeah, yeah..." Joe grumbled.

Now he was in a real pickle. He didn't know what Ventura's consultant might have done.

MOTION DETECTED. PLEASE ENTER CODE.

"Does we have code?"

Joe gritted his teeth. "No, we does not."

"How long is the patience?"

Joe tapped furiously in another document, searching for any override codes that might be applicable. "Of the alarm? Not long."

On cue, the lights in the gallery flashed in a slow strobe. A klaxon blared. "UNAUTHORIZED ENTRY. REMAIN MOTIONLESS AND AWAIT SECURITY. UNAUTHORIZED ENTRY. REMAIN MOTIONLESS AND AWAIT SECURITY…"

"I do not agree," Fooshri stated. "Security guy, make new plan."

"We need to get out of here."

Yanking his datapad, he ripped the cable out of the console. Joe stuffed his tools haphazardly into his pack.

Fooshri beat him to the door. "Let me cut the—"

Joe tried the door controls.

Not only did the door not open, a rain of purple dye sprayed from an array of nozzles in a grid across the ceiling.

"Power," Fooshri finished.

Being doused by criminal-identifying dye barely slowed the laaku. Her plasma torch sputtered as the nozzle got wet but quickly burned away the residue and insta-boiled any more that fell. Fooshri sliced open a secure panel, then took no prisoners severing every connection to the door.

"Pull," she ordered.

Getting a grip on a well-made door was the trick. Slick with greasy purple pigment, neither could find purchase. Muscling her human counterpart out of the way, she cut oval handholds and used gloves to ensure the molten edges didn't burn her.

Joe spared a glance back at the gallery as the pair of them heaved and forced open the door. The dye was ruining expensive furniture and decorative lighting. But the stuff ran right off the display cases, where valueless forgeries stared back unharmed, almost winking at the irony.

"What an absolute madman. He'd risk the whole collection just to *catch* someone trying to steal it."

Fooshri tugged his sleeve from beyond the door. "Much haste. Many washroom. We look very conspiracy grapes."

The datapad on the bedside table buzzed. Its screen flashed red. A pasty, trembling hand flopped toward it ineffectually. A firmer, softer, stronger hand took a wrist, guided it back to the surface of the bed, and pinned it there.

"But... gallery..." The words came as gasped whispers.

Another authoritative hand cupped his chin and forced him to face his captor. She shook her head. "Not important."

Robert Ventura tried to nod in argument, but the hand that held his head wouldn't budge. It covered his mouth. His nostrils flared with each struggling breath. Her weight atop his torso kept his lungs from filling fully.

She reached over and dismissed the alarm.

Even once released, his protest was feeble. "But..."

"Shh," she cooed, caressing his face. "One last big one before I leave. OK?"

She nodded his head for him.

From the bedside, she retrieved the pill bottle.

He flopped his head side to side. "No more." It was barely a croak.

"Yes. Last one. Promise."

She guided a glass to his lips. He drank with resignation, gasping after a single swallow. She shook pills into her hand, outside his field of view, without even counting.

In one swift sequence, she pressed the handful of marital pharma into his mouth, followed immediately by a gulp of water, then covered both his nose and mouth.

Ventura batted at her, tried to pull her hands away, anything to fight back. It was all ineffectual. Flaccid muscles and jittering nerves were no match for his oppressor.

"Swallow," she ordered sternly. "Swaaaa-loooow."

Unable to breathe, Ventura complied.

"There's a good boy." She took her hand away. The greedy lecher sucked desperate breaths.

"You... what... did...?"

She climbed off of him. He attempted to rise to his elbows, but a light shove was enough to collapse twitching muscles out from under him. Ventura's chest rose and fell in heaves. He clawed a hand at his sternum.

"You must eat that stuff like Choc-O-Poofs to have lasted this long. Don't worry, the pain won't linger."

"Doctor... quick..."

She collected her clothes and held them in a bundle as she came to loom over him. "Your major sin was greed, but the one that got you was lust."

"Who...?"

She shrugged. "Don't know if you mean me or whoever hired me. This isn't personal, if that's any consolation. But I suspect you know you deserve it."

Turning her back on her convulsing victim, she took a brisk, efficient shower. Upon her return to the bedroom, she donned a pair of forensic gloves and the skimpy swimsuit she was able to smuggle in with her, nominally to wear home after rendering her services.

It took the better part of an hour, but she cleaned Ventura's apartment of any trace of her presence using supplies squirreled away by his own housekeeping staff. Along the way, she even discovered a spare uniform to put on afterward.

The most unpleasant part of the whole operation was the bed itself. Ventura wasn't dead yet when she started, and the sponge bath he received was as close as he was going to get to that final joyride he'd clearly hoped for. She changed the sheets beneath him, gathered all the clothing either of them had touched, and set the dish processor on a cycle with their drinking glasses.

As she prepared to depart, dressed as a maid and bearing a sack destined for the reactor core, she paused to check Ventura for a pulse.

Nothing.

Staring, lifeless eyes gazed up at his own reflection in a mirror that spanned the entire ceiling.

Appropriate. A man who'd lived for no one but himself had gotten a spectacular view of his own death.

———

Neeta made her way swiftly through the *Convoy Queen*, darting through crowds and using tricks of the ship that few were even aware of. There was a maintenance supply room that had separate entrances opening onto two different concourses. An employee-only lift wasn't actually locked out from general use beyond a simple warning sticker. Most importantly, there was a stairwell up to the upper reaches that led to a ladder back down to the mezzanine level that saved ten minutes of walking for access direct from the main floor.

All of this came as second nature as Neeta tore through the *Convoy Queen* in search of two derelict lookouts.

She didn't know what to expect when she got there. Were Chuck's kid and the young laaku playing cards, watching pirate flatvids on their datapad, or had they completely abandoned their posts?

When she arrived, sneaking up on them from behind a support strut that they should have had eyes on, she instead found them—to all outward appearances—attending their duties.

"Hey!" she snapped in a harsh whisper.

Both human and laaku jumped at the sound of her voice. Jomek fumbled a micro-measuring device used to adjust their camera angles but caught it before it fell into the swap meet far below. Brad lost his grip on his binocs, but the strap jerked taut, and they hung cockeyed from his neck.

"Hi," Brad replied, recovering quickly and donning a smile. He tapped his earpiece. "Didn't get any warning you were coming."

"Surprise inspection. Whatchu two bozos peeping?" There was something suspicious about the directions they'd been staking out. Neither had eyes on the entrance Chuck and Mort were now guarding on foot. They hadn't even given a hint that they knew they'd been cut out of the process. She turned up a palm and beckoned with gloved fingers. "Gimme?"

Brad ducked as he slid the strap over his head and relinquished the binocs. Pushing up her goggles, Neeta tried to recreate the view Brad would have had upon her arrival.

He'd been gazing down into the swap meet...

Horse-kabob stall... nah...

Multi-species shoe store... double-nah...

Hand-carved stone knickknacks... not in this galaxy or any other.

Then she spotted a notorious stall, surrounded by curtains. Of course...

Neeta snorted in derision. "Tasha's Titty Tent? Really?"

If getting caught peeking at naked women—what little was

visible of them, given the obstructed view—gyrating for hardcoin tips from lonely spacers bothered them, it didn't show. "Hey, spend your millions how you want. I'm planning ahead. Not *my* fault they don't have a roof."

"Sure it ain't..."

Brad extended an upturned palm. "Can I have those back?"

"Naw. We got work. Moving time down in—"

"*Shitshitshitshit,*" Joe blurted over all the heist's comm channels.

Chuck was all over it. "*What happened?*"

"*Backup alarm. Purple shit rained down on us.*"

Neeta brought up the binocs and scanned the area leading to the gallery. She spotted Chuck and Mort. The pair were occupying more than their share of space at the swap meet exit that led to the gallery. Had Neeta taken the default route, she'd have slipped right past them in the other direction.

"Don't see no response yet," she reported back.

"Do you feel a shift in the wind?" Brad asked. He wasn't on an open comm, Neeta didn't hear him through the earpiece.

The question struck a chord in the back of Neeta's mind. She glanced up at the nearest life support blower, one of the giant vents that spilled clean air down into the retail space below.

"Warm..."

"Much misfortune. Many wake-ups." Jomek pointed down at the scattering of sitharn guards slumbering on the mezzanine level.

While the purported lookouts might be happy conversing privately, Neeta knew this needed wider attention. "Problem. Dozey lizards gonna be toasty soon. Blow's gone hot again."

"*Navigation prioritizes me. Unable the sabotage more. Beloved assistance?*" Oblek yammered. Fine. He was busy. But half a billion worth of art wasn't going anywhere if the sitharn got their wake on and started locking down the *Convoy Queen.*

"*I am purple.*"

The simple fact that they needed to eliminate the trail of incriminating evidence precluded the other laaku from helping with the environmental controls.

"*Calling an audible,*" Chuck announced. "*Forget the blowers. Focus on the escort. Peanut, find a grav sled. We'll stash the haul with whatever else is on the one you find. Then detour to the hangars. Me, Mordred, and the lookouts will clear a path.*"

Joe piped up. "*Where can we wash off?*"

"*My fur stained. Washing will not enough.*"

Shit. Even if they were totally purple, they couldn't be leaving a dripping violet trail. Neeta needed to find them a discreet washroom, at the least.

Still not on the comm, Brad chimed in. "*EV suits.*"

Damn. That was brilliant. Maybe the kid wasn't a total parking weight after all. "*A'right. Here's the skinny. Bye-bye pods got lockers nearby. Snag a couple outside suits. They got human and laaku. Nearest is a right, third left, another right from the gallery. On it?*"

"*Wait. We already took a couple of—*" Joe began, before Fooshri cut in with a quick, "*On it.*"

"*My mother,*" Jomek said, beaming with pride. "*Much spatial awareness. Many—*"

"*Annoying,*" Neeta finished for him. "*Learn yourself English like the rest of your species.*"

"*See?*" Brad asked. "*This is why I wasn't trying to mate with her.*"

"*Hold up. What?*" Neeta demanded. She lowered her binocs to glare at the kid.

OK. Kid was downplaying him. He was possibly old

enough to fly. He had faint, patchy stubble that suggested he shaved. But he still *sounded* like a kid.

"Eyes on the job, xenoist," Brad replied acidly. He pointed down toward where Chuck and Mort were directing traffic with absolutely no authority to do so. "And for the record, I have no issue with the arm."

Instinctively, Neeta clutched at her cybernetic arm. "How'd you even know? It's silent."

"Cold hands shake. Even with gloves on, your fleshy hand is cold. Never had a girlfriend with a cyber part."

Neeta was as silent as her Phabian-made replacement arm for a moment. Then she turned to Jomek. "Sorry about the crack."

The young laaku smiled. "Much understanding. Many forgiveness. Attention to the job now, please."

With a solemn nod, Neeta turned her binocs back to surveying the scene unfolding below. "Chaplain, Mordred, I got eyes on trouble incoming."

———

An alert blared accusingly across the bridge of the *Convoy Queen*. Red trimmed the upper edge of the chamber like tacky neon crown molding. All security displays reiterated the same message.

UNAUTHORIZED ENTRY IN GALLERY. DISPATCH SECURITY TEAM.

"Any word?" Captain Ticonderoga inquired.

"No, sir. Krislar is holed up in his office with his two lone unaffected officers. They're trying to source sitharn-sized EV suits from the vendors."

"Damn them. Why don't we have suits for all security personnel?"

Ticonderoga knew the answer to his own question. It ran twofold. Firstly, it sent a bad message to the hordes of spacers who came aboard the ancient *Convoy Queen*, retrofitted and refitted so many times that its own designers wouldn't recognize it, that the vessel wasn't spaceworthy. Secondly, and more importantly, it would have cost money that could have been put to better use in Robert Ventura's own pockets.

None of the bridge crew provided a rhetorical answer. They knew it, too.

"Biers, take a couple janitors down there to investigate. Make sure they know the business end of a blaster."

With security and maintenance both completely depleted, that was his next source for raw sentient mass to dispatch.

"Aye, sir," Lieutenant Biers replied with a hasty salute before rushing off to obey.

A comm patched in from an unknown sender, bypassing even the captain's need to accept any missive. *"Accidental crossing of circuits. No need for alarm over alarm. Please thank you to not panic during successful repairs of heat system."* The voice was female and laaku, spoken with a curious accent. In fact, it almost sounded like a ratatoret on a slow-down filter.

"Should we call back Biers?" Grayson asked.

"Negative. Grayson, take a second team and search the maintenance crawlspaces. Something isn't right on this ship, and I suspect it's more than the usual cut corners coming back to slice us in the ass."

Strange that Ventura hadn't already hit the intraship comm to chew Ticonderoga's ass out. For a moment, he considered sending another team to round up their employer. Just as quickly, he decided against it. This whole mess was a chain of dominoes leading back to chronic underfunding and management via accounting ledger. At best, Ventura would be an obstacle to staunching the bleeding; at worst, he might compound it.

Not only that, Ticonderoga strongly suspected that Robert Ventura was already on his way to his precious gallery without a second thought for the crew.

━━━

Lou kept his head down and pushed.

The grav sled was a cheapie model, patched with an off-brand power source and operating on five out of six repulsors. He'd shifted the payload to compensate, not even knowing what the crates contained. Nothing he was carting around right now mattered. The clutter of mismatched belongings the Howling Comets brought to market was just a cover story.

A ragged, broken line of day-work volunteers shuffled along, happy to pocket 100T doing honest work for some of the galaxy's least honest employers. Rough characters with overtly offensive clothing, mannerisms, and language patrolled the convoy rendered in miniature within the larger Ventura vessel, weapons bared casually and with only oblique menace.

"C'mon, you slops. Keep it moving," one coaxed, pinwheeling a forearm while the other hand balancing a blaster rifle on his shoulder, finger poised dangerously on the trigger. "Easy money don't mean free money. Earn your blood."

Lou kept moving, allowing the grav sled its natural veer to the left before overcorrecting to straighten it out again.

Casual gawkers peeked only when the pirates weren't nearby. And given the lengthy string of cargo workers and the paltry number of overseers, that was plenty. Luckily for Lou, he knew from Neeta that the traders were generally on his side. Stealing from the pirates was sport around here, dangerous in the vague general sense, but barrel-fishing for a seasoned operator. The overblown security presence was bluster; the effort of defending a few trinkets and knickknacks was too much work for pirates looking for a visit to the terra machine followed by R & R on some resort planet that didn't ask too many questions.

This was just a necessary chore for them.

For Lou, it was an opportunity.

Once he was sure the nearest pirate didn't have a sight line on him, Lou allowed his grav sled to take a hard left down a side corridor. Out of the corner of his eye, he thought he spotted a silent cheer or two from giddy spectators.

Free from scrutiny, he sped his pace, putting distance between the telltale hum of struggling repulsors and anyone who might hear that noise as out of place.

A few turns took him to the rendezvous point. He pressed a finger to his earpiece. "Cucumber, this is Peanut, I've got—"

The louvred cover above punched free from its vent. Oblek held out a knapsack until Lou extended his hands, then dropped it down. Swinging out of the ducts, the laaku made the three-meter drop to the floor with a grunt and a stretch. "Much age. Many aches. We behoove movement."

"What about the rover?"

Oblek pulled out a remote.

Lou's eyes shot wide. "Is that a *detonator*?"

"Evidence and distraction; who is to say which?" The laaku grinned.

"As a last resort, right?"

Oblek scowled briefly. "Medium resort. Last resort is surrender."

With a snicker, Lou stepped aside and allowed Oblek to pilot the grav sled. He activated his comm and used their code words. "Dead men walking. Cucumber's harvesting the crop."

⊏⊐

"Excellent," Chuck replied to Lou's comm. "Bird's nest, guide them in. We'll hold position a little longer and head for the buffet." He noted with growing dismay this his breath no longer steamed in the cold. The ship was warming up quicker than he would have guessed.

Mort glared as someone tried to make their way down the vacant hallway behind them. Whether he used a nudge of magic or not, Chuck couldn't tell. But the gentleman in the threadbare business suit thought better of his intended route and shifted course.

"How long is long enough?" the wizard asked.

Chuck considered. This whole crowd control operation hadn't been on the agenda. As such, they hadn't measured out routes and estimated travel times. This wasn't a precision operation from the start, but it had grown to the point of playing a concert symphony by ear... as it was being composed.

"Until we get too antsy to stay."

"Gonna have to do better, I think," Mort retorted. "I don't worry easily."

"Clear the way!" someone shouted. A pair of uniformed paramedics rushed through the parted crowd with a grav-stretcher laden with emergency medical gear. "Coming through."

Chuck shied from them, wary of drawing that much attention to himself.

Mort, however, blocked their path and held out a palm. "Hold up. No one gets through here. Orders from the bridge."

"Medical emergency. Move aside," the first paramedic ordered.

The second added, "Who do you think you are?"

That was Chuck's cue. "Temp security. One-day hire. What's the trouble?"

"Big guy's office. Housekeeping commed it in."

Chuck and Mort exchanged a glance. That was opening enough for the medical team to shoulder their way past Chuck and around Mort, not caring one shit for their made-up, short-term authority on the matter.

This could have meant so many things.

If their hired sex provider had slipped up, Ventura could have beaten incriminating evidence out of her—or, more likely, ordered someone else to do so on his behalf.

If their hired sex provider had been stimmed up or doped out, she might have crashed—sad and inconvenient, but not a threat.

If something had happened to Ventura, however, that was a problem.

The whole heist was predicated on a lack of investigation. Joe and Fooshri had already screwed the pooch on this being a complete ninja job. But they'd covered their tracks. This should still just look like a *failed* robbery. But if it coincided with a threat to Robert Ventura personally... well, all bets were off.

Whatever had happened, Chuck needed to know. He needed to be ready for whichever cog in their wobbly clock was springing loose.

Chuck jerked his head. Mort took the cue and fell into step as they rushed after the paramedics.

Brad shivered.

It wasn't the presence of cold that had drawn the reaction. No, it was worse than that. It was the sudden return of warmth that reminded a numbed and acclimated body that frigid air wasn't the only option that had prompted the full-body shudder.

Pulling off a glove, Brad held up a hand, catching the flow of air from the nearest blower vent, a flow their perch had been carefully chosen to provide shelter from. There was no mistaking it, the life support temperature regulation was back online.

He tapped his earpiece. "Hey. It's getting warm up here again. What's the deal with the heat?"

"*Much inevitability. Many haste.*"

"*Roger that,*" Joe replied. His voice echoed with the fishbowl acoustics of wearing an EV helm. "*Me and Handkerchief are beelining to the rendezvous.*"

Neeta muttered something aloud that didn't repeat over the comm channel. "Where the fuck?" Then she switched to group chat. "Yo, Chaplain. Wrong way."

Dad replied immediately. "*All copacetic. Just gotta check one thing. Rally up. We'll be there pronto.*"

"We can't ditch yet," Neeta protested. "Payload's coming."

"*Yessiree,*" Lou reported in. "*We're about 20 seconds inbound to public foot traffic. Wouldn't mind the okie-doke on our route.*"

Dad was all over this. "*Negative. Kiddos can't hold that position if we get a mass wake-up. Recon from ground level and stay ahead of Peanut.*"

"*And Cucumber,*" Oblek added.

"Naw. Can't risk the terra-load. I got this. I'll guide Maverick and Copernicus safe... once the load's secure."

"*Maverick. Get your ass to the rendezvous. NOW! Drag Gremlin if you have to. Or ditch her.*"

Brad gave Neeta a steady look. She'd heard the same comm. Their eyes met. Behind the goggles, the whites showed around her eyes. He jerked his head aside. "Worse fates than a botch job. Let's lay ions. Nothing worth getting slagged over."

Jomek was already packing.

"What about your dad and the wiz?" she countered. "We supposed to spot for them, too."

Brad smirked and looked up from helping his laaku friend break down their surveillance gear. "Oh, *them* I'm not worried about."

———

Becky watched with half an eye on her two little ones as they chopped, colored, and glued on the floor of the living room. Her other eye studied a contraption she'd assembled from a kit purchased on the cheap from a guy who claimed it was part of an ancient Earth ritual.

Clear glass canisters the size of buckets lined the kitchen table. Hoses and tubes ran in and out, connecting the canisters in a configuration Becky checked and rechecked against the diagrams laid out on her datapad.

Rhiannon raced up to her, hands speckled with glitter and bearing streaks and dots from errant marker usage. She held up a prospectus from a real estate salesman hawking asteroid homesteads. Across the picturesque—and entirely bullshit—landscape, and against the backdrop of stars, Rhi had drawn a house and a family of five.

"You like it?"

Becky tousled her hair. "Great job, babycakes."

"What are you making?"

"It smells bad," Mikey chimed in, not looking up from his scissor work. He was cutting around human figures, setting them aside, and cutting mono-colored paper into the shapes of clothing for them.

"Oh, just more grown-up stuff."

"It does smell bad," Rhi agreed with her brother.

"Well, that's just peachy. Since you don't want none of it anyway."

"Where's Daddy?" Rhi asked. "I wanna show him."

"Daddy's gonna be a while. But I'm sure he's gonna flip for it."

Rhiannon beamed.

Didn't take much to make a kid happy. Long as they were healthy and smiling, Becky wasn't doing such a bad job. Not much else to raising a kid once you boiled it all down.

Speaking of boiling, Becky had checked enough that she felt safe turning on the heat. The first canister warmed, and the contents began to boil.

Becky was no cook. She'd skipped the whole tedious process of fermenting stuff herself and picked a couple dud brews that had been languishing in the cargo hold. A few apple slices had been an impulse addition to spike the flavor a little.

As the contents heated, steam chugged its way through the network of hoses. It took longer than she'd imagined, but killing time was justifiable homicide right now. She had her older boys off playing robbers—hopefully without cops. The quicker that shit got itself done and over with, the better she'd like it.

Eventually, a slow drip out the far side splashed into a waiting tumbler. Eager to test the result, she wiped a finger across the spout and sucked it clean.

Nodding approvingly, she mumbled to herself, "This moonshine's got some kick."

The door slid open. Two paramedics raced inside. Perhaps anticipating the need for a hasty exit, neither closed the door behind them.

Chuck didn't hesitate and followed them all the way to Ventura's bedroom.

Mort paused at the doorway, looked both ways, and ducked in after them.

Few public images were available of Robert Ventura, most from when he was a much younger man. But as a guy who'd been coming to Ventura Convoy on and off for decades, Chuck knew the guy when he saw him. To be fair, most of the images of Ventura had been head shots. But the sight of a naked sexagenarian body beneath that head did little to call the man's identity into question.

The medical team crowded around Ventura like a two-man swarm of locusts. Scanners out, they poked and swept and scowled and manhandled.

"No pulse."

"Still warm."

"Get him circulating."

"Neural activity zero."

"He's not dead till I say he's dead. Circulate him while I set up the neuron reset."

Chuck watched in macabre fascination. Could they do it? For a guy that cheaped out on washroom soap and charged for omni access, the paramedics were packing some impressively shiny-new equipment. The words sounded grim, hopeless even, but modern medicine was real magic.

A soft clearing of the throat caught Chuck's attention. Mort raised an eyebrow, then made a slashing motion across his throat.

A lump caught in Chuck's.

This heist hadn't included an assassination. Ventura being

dead didn't help them one bit. In fact, if word got out, that was just going to draw unwanted scrutiny to the whole affair.

Chuck shook his head.

Mort shrugged.

The paramedics worked like demons.

"No good," one of the paramedics declared at length. "Call it in."

Chuck now frantically gestured to Mort with the same slashing finger across his throat.

Mort scowled back in confusion.

Chuck pointed to his comm earpiece, then repeated the gesture.

With a nod and a wink, Mort reassured him.

The paramedic tapped at his datapad. "Huh. No signal."

"What're you two doing here?" the other demanded.

Chuck stepped in front of the wizard lest inexpert lies be told. "We're on the temporary security detail. You guys should hang tight. We'll get word to the bridge. Captain's going to have a bunch of questions, I'm sure."

"Any idea if we still get paid?" the second paramedic inquired.

Ah, top-of-the-barrel medical talent, to be sure. Now that they'd just declared their meal ticket a stiff, their next worry was their bank accounts.

Chuck aimed a finger blaster at the guy as he retreated toward the door. "Operate on a 'yes' for the time being. And if you two step foot out of this suite before we get back, you're suspects one and two. Got it?"

He didn't wait for the response. Chuck ushered Mort out ahead of him and slapped the door control behind them. Keeping his voice low, he warned the wizard. "Look, that's bad news. We've got until these bozos put the pieces together to be off this ship and in the astral." He tapped his comm. "Hey everyone, we've got a... hey, everyone? Everyone, this is Chaplain... Why am I getting a dead-signal tone?"

The annoying, low-pitch hum was an alert that he was talking to dead air.

Mort gave a sheepish shrug. "Sorry. You wanted dead comms. I killed comms. Not exactly precision work. Imagine trying to eat sushi with a pair of cricket bats instead of chopsticks."

As they hustled back toward the swap meet to make their rendezvous, booted feet approached from the oncoming direction.

It was too late to turn back. The sound was already closer than their nearest avenue of backtracking flight. Chuck pressed on, leading the way and trusting to his handy-dandy bullshit-slinging mouth to solve whatever trouble might be on the way.

The pair rounded a corner and ran smack into a couple sitharn. They wore the drab, off-the-rack uniforms of the *Convoy Queen*. Both carried leveled blaster pistols. One held an honest-to-God, fire-on-a-stick torch as a portable campfire.

"Handsss up," one of the sitharn ordered. "Who are you?"

Chuck complied instantly. "We're just taking a shortcut."

Mort remained impassive.

"Sssearch them," the torch-wielder ordered. He jabbed the flame toward Mort. "And you, raissse your handsss. Now."

Mort turned to Chuck. "Sorry."

Flame leapt from the torch, scorching the faces of the two guards. They cried out in agony.

But Mort wasn't done. This wasn't a Salt-and-Skedaddle or a Ganymede Shuffle that Mort was trying to pull here. With a clawed hand, Mort clobbered one of the sitharn so hard his fingers punctured the reptilian skull. Instantly, smoke boiled out of the guard's eyes and nostrils. And to prove it wasn't a fluke, Mort repeated the same trick left-handed on the other.

Allowing two limp bodies to crumple to the floor, Mort flicked away the gore from both hands.

Chuck didn't know where to begin to react, so he started with a "we just killed someone" staple. "Should we, I dunno, hide the bodies?"

"No need," Mort declared. And as he gestured down toward the dead security guards, Chuck saw why. The corpses were aflame inside, charring and crumbling like firewood at the end of a bonfire.

The lights had gone out already, all but the torch, which made an already gruesome scene all the more ominous. Now, an unseen pipe burst and hissed somewhere behind the nearest wall.

"We should probably haul ass."

Mort shrugged. "Lead the way. You're in charge."

Lou jammed hard on the steering bar, forcing the grav sled back onto a straight path forward more times than he dared to estimate. Something must have shifted in the load, or the remaining repulsors must have been fading, because it was growing harder by the minute to keep on course.

Jerking back on the bar, Lou pulled the sled to a halt.

"Inappropriate stopping," Oblek pointed out. "The place is approaching us."

Lou circled to the front of the conveyance and tugged at the cargo, shimming a stack of crates away from the corner supported by the faulty repulsor. "Just lemme... there. Now we can—"

"Hey!" a gruff voice barked. A pall cast over the background hum of commercial conversation that pervaded the swap meet floor. "Where ya think yer headin'?"

Lou froze. "I... uh..." The pirate held a blaster rifle leveled casually toward his groin. He was two meters tall and a meter wide across the shoulders. Without a sniff of assistance from that weapon, he could have ripped Lou in half.

"Much signs. Many confusion," Oblek interjected. "The assistance welcomes us."

If the pirate had any trouble understanding the laaku's contorted grammar, it didn't show. "Oh yeah? Fine. Folla me." The jerk of his head clarified exactly what "folla" might mean.

Swinging the cumbersome grav sled around, Lou folla'd.

Their newfound guide peeked back often, paralyzing Lou with dread.

What was he going to do?

The *Convoy Queen* was nothing if not a kaleidoscope of distractions. At any moment, an opportunity could present itself to—

"Theft!" Oblek cried out. The laaku hopped atop a pile of crates on the grav sled and pointed a finger into the crowd.

At first, Lou thought it was a ham-fisted ruse, but then he noticed two things.

First, one of the stacks on the grav sled did appear to be shorter by one crate than it had a moment ago.

Second, and far more subtle, was Oblek lower-handing a hardcoin twenty into his back pocket.

The illicit buyer—a round-shouldered spacer with long, scraggly hair—turned back, face slack with shock. "But I just—" The rest of his reply was cut short as a blaster shot ripped through the crowd.

Then another.

And another.

"Get back here, ya filthy weasel!" the pirate shouted.

Despite the peril, when the crowd fled in every direction, the contents of the grav sled drew greedy hands like piranhas.

Lou grabbed and lunged, but before he could make heads or tails of the chaos, he was standing there tending to an empty grav sled.

The pirate, having lost sight of his prey long ago, stopped firing blindly after him. He noticed the flat bed that had once supported a fraction of his ship's merchandise, then fixed Lou with a scowl.

Lou took a step back and put up his hands.

"Useless fuck. What're you still doin' here? Git!"

Lou didn't need to be told twice. He turned tail and ran.

As soon as he found a safe haven, a nook that led to a manual staircase, he opened a comm.

"Shit! Payload MIA. Be on the lookout for a—"

"*Paintings have me,*" Oblek cut in. "*The meeting place approaches. Much feet. Many trouble. Let the art divide us and go home.*"

Lou heard the echo of *let the art divide us.* He knew it was just the way Oblek butchered his English, but he couldn't help wondering who might do what now that they were free and clear with half a billion terras in Earth masterpieces.

———

Brad had never shopped at such a pace before. Sure, in some parts of the vast flea market, commerce probably continued as usual. But with blaster fire in the vicinity, this region was a stampede.

None of the three of them were what one might consider ideal travelers for passengers aboard a stampede. Brad had yet to grow into his masculine bulk despite achieving plausibly adult height. Neeta could have slipped between the bars of many a border colony prison cell. And Jomek... Well, the stampede hadn't been born that catered to the ergonomic and safety needs of a species that barely topped a meter on average.

That meant that navigation relied heavily on reading the currents and allowing the flow to carry them in directions that availed them of their destination. Sometimes that required backtracking. Sometimes it required quick jukes to the side in anticipation of shifts in the chaos. Mostly, though, their journey consisted of keeping their feet underneath them lest they be trampled by the uncaring boots of the mob.

Of course, for Brad, being buffeted through the swap meet by forces beyond his control was merely a metaphor for his life in general. And while they were jostled and swept along through the rows of shops and stalls, he kept an eye out for unattended, pocket-sized objects that might need rescuing from the entropy that threatened to land them in less deserving pockets.

He didn't even pay particular attention to his acquisitions.

There would be time for that later—assuming that whole getting-trampled-to-death thing didn't happen.

"Keep up," Neeta ordered, sparing a glance back at her two charges.

"We're still here," Brad assured her, shouting over the din of panic in the air.

He grabbed a gadget off a counter that appeared to have been mid-transaction when the shooting started. It joined a bracelet that might become a gift to a future girlfriend, a thumb scanner that might have stored digital terras in it once they got back to civilized space, and, of course, the pair of amethysts he couldn't get rid of for fair market value.

"Many legs. Much caution."

"I see why blasters aren't allowed," Brad joked.

"*HALT!*" a reptilian voice boomed from overhead. Few halted. Brad and his companions certainly didn't. The now fully awake sitharn guards once more menaced from the catwalks above. One of them spoke through a handheld amplifier cone. *"CCCEASSSE PANIC AND RETURN TO BUSSSINESSS ASSS USSSUAL."*

When that order produced little effect, the sitharn started firing stun shots into the crowd.

As shoppers and traders collapsed in twitching heaps all around, the stampede wised up. Motion didn't stop, but the frantic pace broke.

Neeta looked back. "Keep moving. Don't get clipped."

Brad never had any intention of getting shot. He doubted that marines on the front lines of a shooting war ever *intended* to catch a wad of plasma. Fact was, being in a shooting gallery came with risks.

No sooner had she warned them than Neeta took a stray shot from an indiscriminate volley into the crowd. The shiprat wobbled to a heap of trench coat on the floor.

Brad threw himself in front of her to divert the now-slower-moving traffic. When the pedestrians adapted and treated them as an obstacle to avoid, he knelt and reached behind her head to check for blood. None. The hood of her coat and the strap of her goggles provided at least some protection against the limp impact.

"Get her legs," Brad ordered.

Jomek complied readily. "This does not look the good. Much inappropriate. Many kidnapping."

"Just shut up and move."

He'd seen it done plenty of times in holos. Carrying fallen comrades took many forms. Cradled against a hero's chest or slung over a shoulder required a protagonist with a little more in the way of upper body development. Brad and Jomek were enacting the most common two-person variant, but even then,

Neeta's backside dragged on the floor, and her head lolled at an angle that threatened whiplash.

Nothing to be done. Blaster stuns could last seconds or minutes, neither of which Brad and his friend had to spare. Body mass usually acted as a buffer against lingering effects, which suggested the scrawny thief might be out a while.

Without any safe haven to fall back on, Brad navigated them toward the rendezvous point.

━━━

Joe looked like an idiot running through the *Convoy Queen* in an EV suit. Felt like one, too. There was a stock character in mainstream holovids who ran around indoors like he was expecting a vacuum failure any second. Always played for comedy, Mr. Indoor Spacesuit could be found at planetside conspiracy theory conventions, escorting his kids to a public pool, or engaged in low-impact sports. In slightly more serious works, Mr. Overly Cautious might wear one to indicate he thought a particular ship or space station could be ready to vent its atmosphere, or Mr. Ready-for-Anything could put one on while waiting for an emergency spacewalk that no one else believed would be necessary.

That's what Joe had been reduced to: a walking visual metaphor.

He and Fooshri made quite the pair, a ready-made Galaxy Giggles Network comedy special. He doubted that asshole Chuck could be as funny on purpose as the mismatched pair just hurrying through a crowded starship.

Joe spoke over his comm. "Sorry for the delay. Me and Handkerchief are on the way." His voice echoed weirdly inside the suit's helmet. He'd always considered himself a traveler through the Black Ocean, not a dyed-in-the-wool spacer. But since he was a dyed-in-the-gallery art thief, he was going to have to get used to the disguise.

And, on the off chance that the rickety old *Convoy Queen's* hull gave out, he was dressed for the occasion.

"Who is this? Identify yourself."

Joe pulled up short, eyes wide. Fooshri skidded to a halt two paces ahead of him. They hadn't patched the heist's comm channel through the suits. He'd picked up an intraship comm system and broadcast to the crew of the *Convoy Queen.*

"Um. I'm... Johnson... sir."

"Who the hell is Johnson? What's your employee number?"

Fooshri gestured hurriedly, waving hands and tapping herself on the head. He had no idea what she wanted him to say. Joe had to improvise.

"Who am I? Who are you? What are you doing in my ear? This is the starship..." He tried to remember the name he'd heard thrown around the swap meet. All the traders buzzed about the pirates' arrival. It only too a second to click in his memory. "*Quasar Cannibal.* I've got a mind to—"

Fooshri tackled him to the floor. For a smaller species, laaku were surprisingly dense and notoriously brawny. With a twist that came near to snapping his head off at the neck, she released the seal on his helmet and tore it off.

"Hey!" Joe protested.

But the laaku ignored him. She dug at the innards with a multi-tool. The last thing he heard coming from inside the helmet was, *"Hold your position. We're sending a team to—"* With an electric sizzle, the words cut off.

Cocking back an arm, Fooshri pitched the helmet back into the hallway from which they'd come. Then, she removed her own helmet and did the same with it.

"Bad conversation anyway. We go."

Now able to reach his ear and tap his heist-approved comm device, Joe checked in. "Slight delay. We're on the way."

"*Gonna be a problem,*" Lou reported back. "*All hangars are in full lockdown. We need a bypass.*"

"I go," Fooshri replied over the channel. "Wait for me as you can. Do not be caught." She added something at the end in her own language, then made a kissing noise into the mic.

"Need backup?" Joe asked once the channel was closed for both of them.

She shook her head. "Much quickness. Many stealth. May good luck have you."

They parted ways with a mutual nod.

Despite wearing an EV suit with *no* helmet now, and with his face and hair splattered with purple dye, he felt less idiotic than he had the moment before. He dashed headlong into the throng of traders and swindlers, intent on making it to the rendezvous to receive his cut. Along the way, he couldn't help catching sight of himself in the mirror at one of the clothing outlets.

Maybe he'd find the time to at least shoplift a hat.

<hr />

Bedlam, thy name is *Convoy Queen.*

Chuck couldn't think what old play he was paraphrasing, or which holovid. But whoever had originated the idea, it was never truer than today. Passengers and crews from a thousand ships had representatives aboard the *Convoy Queen.* With temperature controls gone wild, docking berths impossible to come by, and now some asshole discharging a blaster in the swap meet, people had reached their sanity's limit.

Chuck could only hope they stayed crazy and dumb long enough for everyone in the heist to make the getaway.

As he jogged with Mort at his side, skirting the perimeter of the retail space, Chuck reflected on the operation. He'd never headed a criminal endeavor this size before. It suited him. Chaos had broken out, yet he maintained a cool, calm, collected demeanor and had navigated them through an asteroid field of entirely impossible to anticipate troubles.

"Been fun, huh?" he asked the wizard.

"Which part? The pointless yammering, the idle waiting, or the purposeful waiting in the nose-numbing cold?"

"The thrill. The challenge. The uncertainty with the promise of untold success." He had to couch his words lest a random passerby should happen to be affiliated with the ship.

"The pirates," Mort stated.

"Fine, there's that, but they're really just a minor inconvenience in the grand—"

Mort pointed. "I mean those pirates."

A trio of pirates straight out of Hollyworld's dream casting call fanned out across the exit they'd been planning to take to the hangars. Leather. Spikes. Tattoos. Cyber implants. And Saint Eastwood... the shooting irons they were packing.

"Nobody's leavin' right about now. Get yer asses back to buyin'. We're gettin' paid, and that's all there is."

Chuck darted aside and rushed to jam a thumb in this new hole his heist had sprung. So, the pirates wanted all their junk sold before the panicked shoppers fled for the safety of the convoy and parts beyond. Hard to blame them. But an enforced shopping anti-curfew? That was a fresh twist that hadn't come up in the brainstorm.

Whipping out a datapad, Chuck referenced the ship's schematics. If the pirates had one main exit covered, they probably had the manpower to block all of them. That left less conventional passages. If only he'd had any training in engineering or mechanics or architecture or cartography or...

well, anything but comedy and a basic public education, the blueprints might have been easier to figure out.

"What's the sudden interest in abstract art?" Mort inquired, peering over his shoulder.

"It's not art. It's the ship schematics. If you'd been paying attention during the—of course you weren't... Well, I'm looking for some kind of crawlway or ductwork we can maybe crawl through to get out of here."

"I'm not crawling."

Chuck didn't so much as glance up. Would it kill the wizard to sacrifice a little dignity for the sake of expediency? "Fine. But that might narrow down our options to nothing."

"Not nothing." A firm hand clapped him reassuringly on the back. "Put the flatbook away. It was a good try. But it's about time we just got this done."

"Got what? Huh?" Chuck blinked a few times, struggling to snap back to his surroundings and withdraw from the twisted wire-frame hell his datapad was showing him. That's when he realized Mort was casually walking up to the pirates.

There was just a manner about Mort. He had a switch. It flicked from grandfatherly thirty-something vagabond to disrespected Olympian god with shocking ease. Up to now, he'd played along with the heist, planned as a bloodless exercise in exploiting the security weaknesses of a paranoid miser of an art hoarder. But like a barfly opening a tab, now that the first bodies had been counted, there was no point in exercising restraint.

The pirates never spoke a word. As soon as they noticed Mort, they were on fire.

Deck plates creaked and groaned. Ominous hissing deep in the floor told a story of a hull breach. Improperly grounded light fixtures blew sparks as they went out. Chuck's datapad went dark.

He did the only thing that came to mind. Cupping his hands to his mouth, Chuck bellowed at the top of his lungs. "Run for your lives! There's a wizard aboard!"

Then, grabbing Mort on the way, he ran for the hangar, lit by the faint light of three thrashing corpses who didn't yet accept their fate.

———

Brad clenched his fists inside his pockets, not even trying to inventory his minor thefts during the escape.

The *Radio City* was right there. Waiting. Ready. Just the other side of the airlock. Moments ago, he'd even heard the clunk of the magnetic pay-lock release. They could depart whenever.

Three of their number were still unaccounted for.

Fooshri had no doubt been the cause of the ship—probably *all* the ships—no longer being locked behind Ventura's pay-for-docking system.

Dad and Mort were just plain late.

Neeta leaned against the wall, goggles aimed at the door.

Oblek had the knapsack with the loot to be divvied up. Jomek spoke with him in hushed Kejathi.

Lou stood there silent, not taking his eyes off the knapsack.

Joe wore a stolen EV suit and a bolero that didn't hide the fact that he'd gotten drenched with anti-theft dye like an amateur.

They were waiting around like it was the premiere of a new holovid on a barren world that didn't have many entertainment options. Tension filled the small antechamber with the airlock waiting for their decision to depart. It was the finish line, and they were choosing not to cross yet. Brad watched that fact eat at each and every one of them.

Chuck arrived, panting for breath. Mort followed close behind.

"Ship's too damn big," the wizard griped.

"Good," Lou declared. "Let's split the take and get off this barge."

"We wait more," Jomek insisted. "Mother still missing."

The overhead speakers boomed. "*All ships, abandon the hands. Saying twice, all ships, abandon the hands.*" It was Fooshri, without a doubt.

"She's late," Joe declared. He pointed to the two laaku present. "Take your cut. Wait as long as you want. But you heard her. If you don't get out of here, you can't meet up with her at Carousel."

Oblek pointed to Neeta. "You. The ship lives in you. Fooshri the finding. Safe keep. Yes?"

"You're not cutting me out so easy." The shiprat crossed her arms like a barricade against being bullied.

"We're good for it," Chuck assured her.

Not even Brad was buying that. "We are?"

"I'll make sure he keeps his word," Mort swore with the faint ring of an oath to it.

"Yeah? That supposed to cuddle me? Who the fuck are you? And don't gimme the spiel again."

"We can't leave you with one of the paintings," Lou said, looking for support. "Can we? That'll be hotter than a pulsar if it stays aboard."

It was an impasse.

Joe stepped toward Oblek. "Let's just distribute the art. If Neeta wants—"

"Gremlin," Chuck butted in.

Joe threw his arms wide. "Job's over! If *Neeta* wants to risk her cut—"

"I don't."

"No art. Waiting for Fooshri. Much resolve. Many insistences." He pointed to Neeta again. "Guard of the body or not having the booty."

For a laaku who practically boasted of shitty English skills, the turn of phrase struck Brad as clever. He smirked. Then, when his fingers brushed against something in his pockets, he smirked all the wider.

"What's so funny?" Chuck demanded.

Not him. That much was certain. Brad pulled out the pair of amethysts. He held them in his open palm and presented them to Neeta. "Collateral."

"What?" she asked.

"You find Fooshri. Get her safe. Meet us on Carousel. I get my gems back when you get your cut. Collateral."

"Are those even real?"

Mort nodded gravely. "They're real."

Neeta headed for a corner of the room, the most privacy any of them was liable to find. She dragged Brad by the sleeve and pinned him between two walls and her. She was so close their noses almost touched. He went cross-eyed trying to lock gazes with her through the goggles.

"What are these worth?" Her voice was low enough that no one else could possibly have overheard.

"Dunno. More than anyone's willing to offer for them. The only guys even willing to scope 'em begged off not wanting the attention they might bring."

"Then why would I want them?" she demanded.

"Collateral?" Brad suggested lamely. It was the only answer he could come up with.

"If you volunteer to stay, I'll stay. I don't trust your father not to ditch Fooshri."

"Then you don't understand nomads. He'd sooner leave me

than her. They made a deal. Me? He'd chalk it up as a life experience, finding my way back to the ship."

"What if you came back with me. We'd be rich. We could live how we want."

"Thought you hated me."

"Thought you said I was xenoist. We've all been on edge. But the two of us, we've got our future. You're... different from the guys I know. More galactic." She glanced aside, just briefly. "I want someone who knows me before I got money."

Then she kissed him.

As someone who was making a practice of honing his relationship skills—leaning heavily in favor of the physical—he had to rate the kiss as... fine. Technically proficient, if unimaginative. It lacked the desperate explosion of repressed passion he'd found in May or the sensual confidence of Angelica. But neither had it exhibited the weird toothiness of Genevieve, the excessive saliva of Lucile, or the weird meaty aftertaste he'd gotten from Riinka.

Just... fine.

Brad might have been self-aware enough to realize he could act impulsively at times. But even he wasn't impulsive enough to run away from home to live with a nouveau-riche shiprat over "fine."

He kissed her back, of course. It was a cultural obligation. But hiding beneath a trench coat, she'd done little to spark either Brad's imagination or his passions. He gave her a stage actor's version of romance—just going through the motions.

After all, he had an audience.

Neeta looked at him expectantly. Vulnerable. She'd let down her facade of taciturn independence.

Brad pressed the gems into her hand—her real, fleshy hand beneath its glove. "Find Jomek's mom. Keep her safe until the heat is off. See you on Carousel." He planted a kiss on her cheek.

After that, they divvied up the artwork and scattered to their respective ships.

———

Falling water cleansed the tension, soothed raw nerves, and restored a sense of normalcy that had slipped in the previous few hours. Chuck let the scent of cheap body soap fill his nostrils, replacing the smell of burning pirate flesh. It washed off the sweat of panic, the germs from handshakes, the stains of cheap chicken wing sauce.

Chuck's whole trip to Ventura Convoy swirled down the shower drain.

All but the two paintings tucked away in a corner of the cargo hold for safekeeping.

Technically, Wheatfield with Crows was Mort's cut; The Dance Class was in Chuck's custody. But for all practical purposes, both were just expensive dry-cleaning vouchers until they converted them to terras on Carousel.

Shutting off the water, Chuck performed a quick wipe-down before wrapping himself in the damp towel.

He exited the shower grinning.

In the living room, his family gathered in wholesome recreation.

Relieved of primary responsibility for the littles, Becky was drinking tequila straight from the bottle—or, based on the contraption assembled in the kitchen, drinking *something* straight from a tequila bottle.

Brad had the volume cranked to maximum watching a Zenia the Pirate Hunter holo that Mike and Rhiannon shouldn't have been exposed to.

To their credit, the small ones ignored the flashing blasters and splattering alien blood, engrossed in their arts and crafts time. They chopped with safety scissors and glued and painted and marked and folded and did all manner of other child-friendly activities that could be washed off later.

Mort, unsurprisingly, had retreated to his bunk.

A plan formed in Chuck's brain, crystallizing instantly in pure simplicity. He was going to throw on something comfortable to wear, crack open a beer, and commandeer the holo-projector remote.

Done deal. Easy as a Martian girl.

When he emerged from the bedroom in a baggy tracksuit and house slippers, Chuck headed straight for the fridge. Their beer supply had been picked over, but he'd made sure to stock up at the convoy before getting sidetracked ensuring the Ramsey family fortune for generations to come.

Moseying through the wasteland of uncapped markers and hacked-up plastisheet, he headed out to the cargo hold for a reload. Nobody selling at Ventura had been packing *good* beer, but Chuck wasn't in the mood for good. He wanted familiar, comforting, a reminder of what life was like as a working stiff. He promised himself something right then and there.

"I'm not gonna be one of those rich assholes who insists the money hasn't changed them. I'm gonna be right upfront about it."

He'd drink all the shitty booze on board—there'd be no shortage of help on that count—and from that point forward, it would be nothing but the best.

Cradling a case of Hapsburg Stout against his belly, he was almost to the door before an impulse forced him to set it down.

He had to check.

There was no one on board the *Radio City* he didn't trust. There hadn't been one of those last-minute scrambles to escape that resulted in shady strangers bunking on his ship. The crew consisted of nothing but shady family—Mort included—that Chuck trusted with his life and his money.

Yeah. Even Brad.

Chuck just wanted to see the paintings again. Personally, Wheatfield with Crows and The Dance Class did nothing for him. Neither did any of the Old Earth flatpics the others held as insurance of their cuts. To him, it looked like an asteroid all his own, servants and mistresses, a luxury yacht for every day of the week, and hot and cold champagne running from the faucets.

Except...

"Where'd they go?"

Chuck shifted boxes and crates, gently leaned the tennis table aside, and crawled on the floor to check under anything that *had* an under.

A horrible, horrible thought crossed Chuck's mind, and he couldn't shake it until he checked to make sure.

Racing back to the living room, he fell to his hands and knees beside Rhi and Mikey.

"Daddy, see what I make?" Rhi asked. She held up a flower-petal cutout with a pink bee scribbled in the center.

Chuck's eyes spotted several other cutouts of similar shape and decoration. On his other side, Mikey more deftly traced images of ballerinas with scissors.

"It's... swell... baby," Chuck's brain answered on autopilot.

Two priceless masterpieces, each about to acquire a market value on lawless Carousel, lay in tatters. With low estimates projecting one hundred million terras apiece, they'd been sacrificed on the altar of developing fine motor skills and expressing creativity.

Still in shock, Chuck stared at his wife, semi-comatose on the couch. "How could you let them...?"

"Chill ouuuuuuut," Becky assured him languidly. "They ain't real. The ones you 'bought' are still groovy."

Chuck picked up the large remnant of Wheatfield with Crows with its holes and the access cuts leading to those holes. "But... these *are* the ones we stole."

Becky's shoulders shook before the laughter erupted like a slow volcano. "Naw... them old painters didn't have plastic. I may not know art. But I know plastic's newer than them masterpieces. I'm no fool. I checked. Damn right, I checked."

Struggling to process, Chuck squinted at the cut edges.

She was right.

"Plastic..." he echoed hollowly. Then, as anger rose up inside him, he shook aside his confusion and resolved himself.

Storming over to the couch, Chuck confiscated the remote.

"Hey!" Brad snapped, pulling himself free of the holovid's clutches as Chuck shut it off. "I was watching that."

"Hey, *lookout*, were you watching when someone double-crossed us?"

Brad clamped his mouth shut. He scooted from the couch without ever standing upright and disappeared into his room.

Chuck returned to the holo-projector's main menu. "Time to make a video comm. I'm gonna get some answers, and I'm gonna look some bastards in the eye when I get 'em."

———

After several minutes fiddling with settings, checking and rechecking comm IDs, and making bland promises to keep everyone hanging around, Chuck finally had the holovid call ready to rock.

He straightened up, stretched out a kink in his back, and double-checked for any unauthorized audience members. Becky had the kids out in the cargo hold playing some hide and seek with the door to the rest of the ship locked tight. Brad and Mort waited on the couch for the conference to get started—they'd been part of the heist and had as much right to answers as Chuck.

Well, Mort had a right to answers. Brad's presence was mostly honorary.

With the click of a remote, three sets of images popped up. Lou, Joe, and Oblek and Jomek appeared above the Ramsey family holo-projector. Each instantly glanced in random directions, each seeing their own version of the tableau from different angles relative to their respective cameras. Joe was just a floating head. Lou could be seen from the chest up and wore mechanic's coveralls. The two laaku sat in the pilot and copilot's seats of *Otoko Feth*.

Chuck stood at military ease, remote clutched out of sight behind his back. He'd kept the tracksuit on as a stark contrast to the business suit that had been stifling him the whole heist.

"You've got a lot of nerve, Ramsey," Joe led off. "Considering this was *your* plan."

Chuck pointed to himself. "My plan? *My* plan? Who drops out of orbit with a too-good-to-be-true job that turns out to be just that?" He jabbed that same finger at each of them in turn. "I don't know who ended up with the genuine article, but if any of you asteroid mine salesmen show up rich in the next *ten years*, I will make it my personal mission to make sure you pay."

"Same goes for you, Chuck," Lou shot back. "Family's family, but blood is blood. And even blood maybe isn't enough sometimes. For all we know, it was Brad."

Chuck scowled back at his boy. "I know he's got it in him. But Mort's vouched for him. And if anyone on the job needs the money *less* than Mort, I don't know who it is."

Joe was shaking his head. "To be honest, I didn't like having him involved in the first place. I hear the whole convoy's headed for green-sec space and a real investigation. Ventura died of a pleasure drug overdose, but there are bodies. And witnesses."

"Witnesses are never a concern," Mort replied coolly. They both knew that forensically available bodies would be in short supply. Sure, folks probably died in the chaos, but anyone Mort disposed of were beyond serving as evidence.

"Anyone heard from Neeta?" Lou inquired. "Be nice to hear her take on this."

Oblek nodded. "Very recent. Much thankful. Fooshri is picking up us from the passenger transport two days later than now. The words were honest from Neeta."

Chuck sighed. "At the very least, one of us should let her know she's getting screwed along with the rest of us."

Joe scoffed. "Go ahead and stand where they're shoveling, Ramsey. My money's on the laaku."

Chuck cocked his head. "How's that, exactly?"

Taking a deep breath, Joe told his version of what might have gone wrong with the Great Ventura Art Robbery.

━━

It's like this, see? Oblek was up in those vents for too long, unattended, unsupervised, out of sight of everyone else in the heist. Better yet, he had accomplices he knew he could trust.

We came up with our plan, but he was already launching a counterplan inside it. You see, we took a risk concentrating all our technical skills in a clique. Fooshri patched into the security systems. Oblek sabotaged the life support. Even Jomek was responsible for the surveillance tech.

While Lou was off getting the fake prints, Fooshri's using a pirated omni connection to look up what those paintings look like and finding another supplier on board who might have equipment to dummy up her own versions. They don't have to be good because they don't have to fool Ventura—they just have to fool a bunch of dumb humans.

Jomek makes sure that nobody notices them running the prints in from the swap meet; it was easy since all he had to do was casually point out the titty tent to get Brad out of the picture. That's another strike on you, Ramsey, putting your kid on a critical job like that. But even then, odds were slim that anyone but the sharpest-eyed lookout might notice.

So, Oblek's sitting up in the guts of the ship with his own copies of the paintings. He passes Lou's copies through as planned, but when the real ones come back, he swaps them for the second set of fakes.

Conveniently, the toy rover got hung up in both directions. That was the cover story. If it only snagged on the way back, we'd have gotten suspicious. So he fakes the snag heading to the gallery as an alibi.

Here's the trick. He leaves the real masterpieces up there. Just... right in the vents. He didn't have time to do anything else, since Lou was waiting for him at the drop-off. So he signals the missus. She's covered in dye, looking dopey in an EV suit— that shit took five showers to get out, by the way—but she heads to the spot to pick them back up.

Sure, we sicced Neeta on her, but Fooshri's smart. All laaku are smarter than they let on. I haven't worked out exactly how, but I bet those paintings show up at a package delivery and pickup depot on some pre-arranged colony in the middle of the borderlands. We can search them, search their ship, scrub their datapads—they'll have their tracks covered and be squeaky clean.

But just you watch. One of these days, there are going to be some colonial laaku buying a condo on the three-hundredth floor of some Phabian luxury tower.

Chuck blinked in the aftermath of Joe's tale. "Wow."

"Much storytime. Very fiction," Oblek replied.

Joe chimed in. "Hey. No offense, buddy. But you gotta admit, you maybe *could* have done it that way. The facts work."

"No, the facts don't," Jomek interrupted. "False facts are false. Not facts. Mother has talked at me. Father has talked at me. Much comms. Many deductions. I have all facts. I will tell. To start, we have the troubles with terras when on—"

Chuck put up a hand. "Gonna stop ya right there. Super short version. Just a punchline without a joke."

"Much discrimination. Many unfriendship," Oblek said, shaking a finger toward no place in particular. "The story tells itself from a stranger human and has very longness. Too big a longness. And a wrongness. Even a bigger wrongness than longness. Jomek... all the story now."

Jomek shrank in his seat, self-conscious. "Fancy spray peels off. Real paintings copied themselves. Sleight the human hands. Paintings all shrinky. Hide in a pocket."

A silence lingered. Chuck, expert breaker of socially awkward ice, cleared his throat. "Well, we're all a little smarter for having heard that theory. But I'm still not sure we've gotten to the bottom of this."

Lou spread his hands. "Do you mind?"

"Mind what?" Joe asked.

"I have a theory. I think it needs to air out a little. And I don't want any hard feelings over it."

Chuck scoffed. "Well, you're sure making a great case for not hearing it."

"Speaking is acceptable," Oblek insisted. "More speaking. Not less. The bottom has not gotten us, right?"

"Fine," Chuck snapped. "But if you wanna suggest I had anything to do with the scam..."

———

Nah, Chuck, I don't think it was you. But I think you're kinda responsible.

It's Mort.

Sorry, but I just don't buy this "bored wizard just in it for kicks" routine. I know you're buddy-buddy with this guy, but he's some Old Earth aristocrat. Why slum with you and the fam when he can buy himself the lifestyle to which he was accustomed?

And if you want my take on it, on how he did it, I've got one word for you: magic.

Yeah. That's right. He said up front he could pull this whole job himself if he didn't care about making a racket. And guess what? We ran out of there ahead of the panic over a wizard running amok and breaking down the whole damn hull of the *Convoy Queen*.

He didn't just admit it, he rubbed our noses on the floor ahead of time, then pissed there later.

Mort used magic time and again and just made everyone forget. He whammied us, whammied the paintings, whammied the sitharn guards. Do you all really think they're *that* sensitive to the cold? I don't know any sitharn personally, but that seems fishy. But you add magic to the mix, it sounds pretty plausible all of a sudden.

And they claim that Ventura kept a wizard on the payroll. Mort was a bigwig. Probably pulled rank and got the guy to help him. Maybe fed him all the info he needed to make the double-cross run smoothly.

All eyes were drawn to Mort, though no one wanted to look at him with anything that might be construed as a challenge in his eyes.

"Wasn't me," Mort replied to the charges levied against him. "Although I will admit to having a brief chat with Ventura's kept man."

"You never mentioned that," Chuck protested.

Mort shrugged. "My part of the heist had a lot of downtime, especially before it all went octopus-shaped near the end. But I wasn't in cahoots."

"How can you prove it?" Lou demanded.

"He's dead."

A shiver ran up Chuck's spine. "Well, enough for that theory. Please believe me—and I say this as a dear friend of the man. If Mort wanted to take those paintings for himself, he wouldn't have left anyone to gripe about it. It's not like he's got a reputation to worry about."

"Hey!" Mort protested.

Chuck couldn't spit the words out fast enough. "I mean, your whole reputation *is* that you're a killer. What would you lose by offing anyone who got in your way? You *just* admitted to a murder."

Mort shook his head. "When *I* kill wizards, it's not murder."

Chuck wasn't about to get into a moral or linguistic debate, and he was certainly in no position to argue the Convocation's legal glossary with the man. "Fine. But can we all agree that Mort's off the table as a suspect?"

"I have something to contribute," Brad called out, raising a hand. It was a habit he'd no doubt picked up from those planetside schools.

Chuck gave a pleading look to his co-conspirators.

It was Joe who signed their sentencing document and condemned them to a rasher of nonsense. "He was there. Let's just hear him out."

———

OK. Before you shout me down, hear out my whole theory.

We were never supposed to steal those paintings. We were the distraction.

...

What do you *mean* "for what?" For Ventura's assassination. That's what. We sent a hired someone to have sex with him. It was supposed to be the distraction to keep *him* from interfering with *us*. But what if we were the chaos to provide cover for a murderer to poison him with Aphrodite or whatever it was he was on? Wait, is that the girl drug or the guy drug? Doesn't matter. What's important is that Ventura was murdered, and we were never meant to get away with the paintings.

Think about it.

We disabled the security force—or at least crippled it a while. We fucked up the life support. Sent the mechanics on a wild moose chase. Turned off all the cameras. Started like three different riots. I think Dad and Mort even mugged the paramedics who might have saved him.

We were the perfect patsies.

If we'd gotten away with those paintings after all the attention we'd drawn, we'd have been marked for death as soon as they turned up. In fact, Mikey and Rhi cutting up one of the fakes probably kept us from walking into a trap set to eliminate us as witnesses.

It was the perfect crime. The newsfeeds are even calling it an accidental death.

Chuck rubbed his chin. He hated the very idea that there had never been a heist to begin with. That all his planning had been window dressing on an elaborate distraction.

"No. I refuse to believe it. No one would go to *that* much trouble to kill a guy. And I don't mean the effort or expense, that stuff's fine. People have gone all Count of Monte Cristo to get revenge before."

"Great," Mort grumbled. "You've gone and made me hungry."

"But it's how *convoluted* it all would have been just to kill an unlikeable old man. Hell, whoever declared the death accidental probably covered up the murder just so whatever prostitute did the job wouldn't get in trouble. Probably did the examiner a favor."

"Karnobanto of Foothar's Reduction," Oblek stated firmly. When no one responded beyond a unanimous chorus of furrowed brows, he attempted to clarify. "Simple answers best."

Lou snapped his fingers. "Occam's Razor. That's the human version. And yeah, I'm with Obie on this one. A real killer could have just skipped the whole heist part and gotten a —what did Neeta call them?—a 'prossy' to dose him."

Mort snickered.

"What's so funny?" Chuck asked, almost dreading the answer but growing exasperated as the loose ends multiplied.

"You want a simple solution?" Mort asked.

Chuck sighed. "Sure. Any objections?"

No one objected. Even scattered across distant starships, they didn't deny the wizard.

Mort cleared his throat elaborately, then stood and tucked his hands into the pocket of his Sigma Slashers sweatshirt.

Young Bradley has demonstrated the absurd extreme of planning on behalf of our theoretical villain. I would contend that the polar opposite is far more likely.

We ended up with fake paintings because that's what was on display in Ventura's gallery.

Oh, I hear the objection. Good authority that he purchased X, Y, and Zed on the galactic art black market. Irrelevant. Whether he owned originals or not, whether he hired a forger or bought one of Lou's paint-it-yourself robots, Robert Ventura did not display priceless artwork in that gallery.

I worked for years in a library that kept all its best and most interesting volumes behind lock, key, and guardian.

If I were a wealthy despot of capitalist leanings and bourgeois pretension, I might prefer to own things more valuable than I could affordably protect. So why expose them to risk? If I can display convincing fakes, I fool my guests and I still know I own the real thing. After all, what's a better way to safeguard a piece of artwork, an impregnable fortress built by Hephaistos himself or simply not telling anyone where you put them?

Fakes are cheap in comparison.

Joe and his tawdry little science alarm company was yet another ruse. Because if you don't *pretend* you care enough to defend something, who's going to believe they're the real McCoy?

Anyway, that's my theory. We're the woodpeckers who hammered their faces against a light post and got wires instead of bugs.

Chuck wiped a hand down his face as the wizard finished laying out his theory.

"No."

"It's just a theory," Mort said with a shrug. "Pretty good one, if I do say so myself."

"No. We didn't just run a whole heist to boost plastisheet fakes when there were never real ones to find," Chuck insisted.

"We had *you* case the gallery and list the paintings," Joe pointed out. "If they were fakes, it was on *you* to spot that."

Mort harrumphed. "Told you up front I was no expert. You just needed someone who could tell a da Vinci from a Warhol and had the chops not to fall to pieces chitchatting with a fellow who employs his own little army. You picked me because I was the kind of kid who got to touch the paintings when he toured the Louvre. Not just because they ward them against fingerprints, but because my parents got their way, and so did I. You needed the chutzpah. You needed the pedigree. You needed my real name. And if, at the end of the day, you employed those resources in pursuit of a bunch of glorified wallpaper, then it was a colossal misuse of my considerable talents."

Chuck let the rant drip off his feathers like he had a coat of down.

Joe, less so. "Fuck you, you crusty relic of the Dark Ages! Maybe if you'd spotted the problem in the first place, we could have figured out where he hid the real ones or called the whole thing off!"

"You gonna let him talk to you like that?" Brad asked quietly enough that the comm might not have picked up the audio.

Mort shrugged. "Why not? *His* words are harmless."

This wasn't getting them anywhere. They didn't have the paintings, just recriminations.

"Hey, at least Mort's way, no one stabbed us in the back," Lou suggested. Considering he was the one who'd bounced around accusations of Mort swiping the true masterpieces, it was a sign of conciliation at last.

"One circle. Many knives. All the stabbings our own backs," Oblek suggested, then he and his son broke into identical laughs.

It didn't fit. The pieces just didn't fit. They were all overlooking something that would make *all* the facts fit, not just a select few. When the piece they were forgetting about fell into place, Chuck broke out in a grin.

"Shut up, you idiots. I'm gonna tell you how this all went down."

There's only two of us not here right now. And just between you, me, and the color purple, I'm willing to bet the title to the *Radio City* that Fooshri wasn't the one with the hidden agenda.

Neeta.

She was our handy, all-purpose, local expert shiprat. Had a guy who could tailor Mort a classy suit on short notice. Knew where the maps and schematics didn't match the actual ship. She found us a caterer, cold-weather supplies, and even the prostitute we didn't feel like cutting in for a full share.

And we never background-checked her. Why would we? The idea of paying for omni access to run the ID of a kid who probably didn't even have a birth record on file... C'mon. Talk about a waste of resources on an already tight timeline.

We were schmucks. We got suckered.

While I think Brad was barking up the wrong tree about the whole murder plot thing, he might have been onto something. We *weren't* the heist. We were the marks.

The lot of us brought in skills that are probably hard—no, impossible—to find in the general population of the convoy. Certainly not among the permanent residents. Joe, you're intimately familiar with a niche security system. Mort's one of the most dangerous wizards in the galaxy. Oblek and Fooshri would be living easy planetside if they spoke newsreader English, probably working for some big engineering firm. And so on...

But Neeta had her own crew.

Why didn't she make a bigger stink about that "prossy" getting a cut? To keep that tiny fraction extra of a fortune none of us could hope to spend?

Or because she was already *getting* a cut of the real payoff. Neeta's payoff. When Joe accused Oblek of faking the rover getting stuck, what if he wasn't faking? What if it was stuck, not because of a minor error in calculation or old ducts being a little out of whack? What if it got stuck because someone reached in and jammed it?

Oblek, you said you were navigating by wheel rotation; you didn't have a camera to steer by. And in a duct, what good would a camera even do, really?

Except see a hole overhead, pre-cut by someone waiting for it.

Someone who knew the plan.

Someone with another set of fake paintings ready and waiting.

Even if they weren't good fakes, they were good enough to fool us. Neeta must have known people who could do a quick print job. Down-on-their-luck mechanics owed her favors—the major currency in any subculture enclave.

Once Oblek had the second set of fakes in hand, the rest of her plan was just getting us off the *Convoy Queen* without her. She had no intention of coming to the rendezvous on Carousel to meet our buyer. Hell, she probably set the buyer up in the first place.

Her end game was having the paintings all to herself with us off trying to fence forgeries.

We'll probably never see her again.

———

"I gave her my gems," Brad said sullenly. He was the first to process Chuck's ion storm revelation.

Chuck laid a hand on his son's shoulder. "I know, son. She took all our gems."

The boy jerked away from the touch. "Fuck you. I mean for real. She took actual, valuable gems I offered as collateral. Tried to get me to stay behind as a hostage, too. I can only imagine what she'd be doing with me right now if I'd agreed."

"Wasn't your call, sport." Chuck tousled the boy's hair. Kept him from getting too big for his britches.

"Even if that was really what happened, what do we do about it?" Lou asked. "Nothing kid like that, she can vanish and show up halfway to the core. Sell the paintings for a tenth their value to someone off the beacons, and she's set for life. New name, new look, private security."

"Quick action. Much haste. Many diligence," Oblek agreed.

Joe waved a hand to gather everyone's attention. "Whoa, hold up. Check the news feeds."

"Any one in particular?" Lou asked.

Joe looked offscreen, fingers tapping. "I'm relaying the feed ID. Screw that. I'm patching it in."

An additional participant joined the multi-way comm. It called itself Art News Hourly. A stuffy-looking host in a tweed skirt suit and wire-rimmed datagoggles spoke with an Old

Earth accent. Joe had patched them into a live feed mid-sentence.

"...*are calling it the art recovery of the decade. Five Earth-origin works ranging from the Renaissance to the Early Data Era were recovered in a daring raid organized by Catskill Shulman Insurance Group. According to a company spokesman, the pieces were part of an illegal private gallery kept by Robert Hubert Ventura, a wealthy recluse who operated a roving black market known as Ventura Starway...*"

Chuck threw up a palm in exasperation. "They even got the name wrong!"

"I like it," Mort commented with a shrug. "Convoy is such a milquetoast word. Evocative of nothing. It's like naming a ship *Ship*. Don't tell me what it is; tell me what it—"

"Can it, pointy-hat," Joe snapped. "I know, depending who we sold to, those paintings could have ended up in an Earthside gallery or as some Martian gangster's dartboard. Who gives a shit? But some goddamn insurance company? That's who tossed us for a vacuum skinny-dip?"

"That's how it sounded from here," Lou replied with a slow bob of his head. "But it's your feed, so don't mind me if I go digging on my own to cross-check."

"Verified," Jomek reported, waggling a datapad as his father scowled in silent agreement. "Same facts. Many places."

Chuck heaved a sigh. "Well, there's no easy way getting those little canvas magic carpets back to ride them to Easy Street. Not anymore." He combed fingers through his hair, shook his head, and paced. "You know, I'd give half what we lost on this job just to know how they did it."

━━━

But here's what really happened.

Six months earlier, a young woman sat down across the desk from Lucinda Palmer of Catskill Shulman Insurance Group. The visitor looked out of place, a malnourished sort of thin on a core world where no one went hungry, threadbare while surrounded by expensive business suits, paranoid despite being utterly safe. Her host was pressed and molded to core life. Blue pantsuit. Dye-blonde bob. Tasteful jewelry. Firm handshake.

Mrs. Palmer tapped a spot on her desk, angled away from the visitor but presumably a data screen. "We're now recording."

"Do we have to?" the visitor asked.

Mrs. Palmer nodded with a reassuring smile. "Company policy. Now, please state your full name."

"Anita Erica Esposito-Ventura. Last bit's new." She grinned. "I had a hunch."

"Miss Esposito-Ventura, we have received—"

"Just Neeta. Ain't formal where I'm from."

Mrs. Palmer indulged and started again. "Neeta, we have received the results of the comparative DNA test. Despite being a 30-second test, obtaining the parental DNA sample required more datawork than usual."

"Yeah, old man's got himself way off the lanes, if ya know what I mean." She gazed out the window at the Martian cityscape, not even sure which city this was or what it mattered. The whole planet was one big city. "Ain't sure why. This core business is tight."

"Be that as it may, I am pleased to inform you that the test came back positive. You are the biological daughter of Robert Hubert Ventura."

Neeta shrugged as she stared out the window at the casual luxury enjoyed by billions of sentients. "Yeah. Figured. No reason for Mom to lie about that limp wreck knockin' her up. Not when she didn't try to get nothing' from him."

"Indeed. However, despite your questionable guardianship status, our legal department assures me that you could successfully sue for seventeen years of paternal absence as well as ongoing financial support until you reach majority."

"Slick."

"However, given the certainty of legal pushback from Robert Ventura, this will incur some middling expense."

"Which I don't got. Roll it. I have the score. Keep the ball moving."

Mrs. Palmer clasped her hands and leaned across her desk. "You've indicated that you can both locate Ventura Starway and secure the safe return of several works of historically significant artwork."

Neeta shrugged. "Yeah. If I had money, I'd have just gone straight for a lawyer. But I got what *you* need, so we can deal. You get me coin for my shitty childhood, I'll cough up some pictures."

They shook hands on the deal.

Three weeks before the heist, Neeta sat at a public access terminal, leaking her last terras into paying for the data service.

She'd never been fishing in her life, but she'd heard about the activity. Parked next to natural water. Bait dangling in the water. Some unsuspecting creature gets hungry and lazy and clumsy and gets got. The Black Ocean was larger than any body of water, and the fish seemed either too cautious or too dumb to notice her tasty bait.

Art.

Paint on cloth.

Dumb as the idea was that ancient Home Arts kiddie projects could be worth more than a starliner, facts were facts. Rich dipshits paid out the ass for art.

Sooner or later, someone would bite.

It had to be sooner. Catskill's lawyers had been clear on one fact: Neeta being underage was key leverage for getting support payments. When the whole process began, an eighteenth birthday felt light-years away. She was now down to mere months, and the war chest she'd saved for this effort was drying up.

She had her team.

She had her plan.

All she needed were key components.

On November 9th, 2541, her luck changed. A disgruntled ex-employee of Iron Moon named Joseph Johansson—either an alias or parents who hated him—contacted her with a request for the location of Ventura Convoy. The finder's fee for the coordinates put her back in business.

———

Five days later, Neeta found herself trailing a young punk through the swap meet. Word down the pipes was that this one was connected to a nomad con man who knew just about everyone. He was the missing link to getting Joe Johansson his heist crew. Chuck Ramsey was his name, and without someone like him, Joe wasn't getting far. Neeta had baited her hook for a master criminal but had caught tech support instead.

Luckily, she hadn't needed to make introductions. Joe started piecing together his own team even before he arrived. When her people caught up with him, he'd already assembled a working core. The risk now became getting shut out of her own plan. Joe didn't know her, and she didn't want anyone tracing the job back to her.

She needed an in. Her in was Brad Ramsey.

The younger Ramsey was a gawky teenager with a shaggy hairdo and wispy stubble. He was lookie-looing the stalls, ogling the shop girls, and pawing at the undergarment racks. Every tech gizmo or patch of exposed female skin dulled his awareness of the galaxy around him. All Neeta had to do was slip his datapad out of his pocket, clone his contact list, and get Chuck Ramsey's ID.

She could have *found* Ramsey the Elder any time she liked. What she needed was proof of her usefulness, her resourcefulness, her indispensableness.

A quick bump and grab of Brad Ramsey caught nothing but air.

What kind of kid walked around without a datapad in his back pocket these days? She'd been confident enough that she'd slipped a hand under his jacket without even confirming one had been there.

A mistake.

Brushing off the incident as casual contact in the cramped crowd, Neeta kept her feet moving. Twiggy and alert, she was the ideal species for slipping upstream against the traffic. Covered head to foot, she'd be impossible to identify if he lost sight. Hood down, goggles off, she'd be a different person. Even her trench coat was a different color on the inside, able to be reversed at a moment's notice.

She never got that moment.

Dammit.

For whatever damn reason, the kid had not only picked her out from among the potential pickpockets in the crowd, he'd gotten it into his head to chase after her.

This was her turf. Her ship. Her home. Neeta wasn't going

to let some spacer kid nab her. Not only did she dread a physical confrontation and having to explain to ship's security why this kid grew a knife out of his belly all of a sudden, but she also still wanted to get on the crew his old man was assembling.

Up and down the rows of stalls, Neeta just planted meters between her and the surprisingly swift teenage busybody. Glances back kept tabs on him until she finally shook sight of him.

That was when she spotted another known member of Ramsey's crew.

No one who'd spied on the newcomers had put a relationship together for the tall, scruffy human in the ragged sweatshirt. Neeta guessed brother-in-law, since he and Ramsey looked nothing alike. But just sharing a ship with the guy was a good indication that *his* datapad would have an ID for Chuck Ramsey as well.

Neeta wasn't too proud to change her plan on the fly. So, she slipped up on the kid. Big whoop.

As she angled for an approach on Ramsey's sweatshirt-wearing crewman, the kid came out of nowhere. Catching Neeta off guard, he wrapped her in a bear hug and plowed her backward through the crowd.

"What the—?"

"Not him!" the young Ramsey insisted in a harsh whisper. "Anyone but him!"

Neeta reminded herself that she wasn't supposed to know who either of them was. She struggled loose from his grasp rather than reach for a weapon. "Who the fuck do think you are?"

Soon enough, she found out.

Neeta had just come from the Big Boring Meeting that took every aspect of robbing Robert Ventura and sucked the fun out of them one by one. Every last one of her fake co-conspirators was exasperating.

Lou loved to re-ask questions that someone had already answered, sometimes more than once.

The laaku were the only members of their species Neeta had ever met who didn't speak better English than her. On top of that, they tried to explain tech stuff like it was anyone else's job to understand that shit. One or the other would have been bad enough, but it hurt two different parts of her brain at once trying to follow along.

Joe had one skill to contribute to the whole plan—and it was a doozy—but he kept bringing up his job at Iron Moon like it made a difference in literally any other aspect of the heist.

Brad might have been cute with his Robin Hood complex if he didn't consider himself to be the prime poor person to receive ill-gotten riches. He treated the whole endeavor as a game, making all kinds of wild claims about what he wanted to do with his half-share of the take.

Mort might have seemed the least overtly offensive of the group, mostly because he largely minded his own business. But Neeta had never dealt with a *real* wizard before. She'd met mercs, marines, and pirates, comet-cold killers who threw around their toughness and willingness to kill like a badge of honor. None of them scared her like the eons-old look in the eyes of a man who didn't shoot people or knife them but instead merely asked the universe to murder people—*and the universe said yes.* Just being in the room with him gave Neeta the creeps.

Worst of the lot had to be Chuck. Credit where credit was due, he put together a crew. But a mastermind he wasn't. And the talking. Talking. Talking. No one could make a comment, ask a question, or answer one without Chuck Gift-to-the-

Galaxy Ramsey putting in his two terras on the matter. Nothing the man said with a ten-minute speech couldn't have been shortened to a sentence or two of straight talk.

Now she was free. This was her part of the plan. She was outside orbital control.

First thing she did was meet up with Cammin. He scrounged her an armor vest, elevated boots, and a targeting helmet with a darkened visor and voice scrambling.

Fifteen minutes after leaving the Chuck-and-Joe comedy show, Neeta was a different person entirely. Leaving her daily wear with Cammin, she headed over to the skin depot.

Whether she grew more jaded by the year or the sex worker district of the ship grew more crowded, Neeta couldn't tell.

Adopting a heavy, lumbering gait, she ignored the entreaties of nightly escorts from every sector of the gender grid. Concealed in her armor, they were all just guessing at her preferences, fishing as much as she had with Joe, except their bait was their bodies and a bevy of lewd promises.

It dirtied her down to the soul, but Neeta had an image in her head.

In the more upscale section of the district, she found what she was looking for. Sporting a busty figure and perfect smile that only cosmo could explain, this one was a dead ringer for Maisie Esposito—Neeta's mother.

"YoU," Neeta said, speaking slowly and trying her damnedest to keep shiprat slang and diction out of her scrambled voice. "CoMe WiTh Me."

"Not even asking the price?" the prossy asked coyly, already flirting for her fee. "I like you already."

They ducked into a nook that found common use for these kinds of negotiations, the ones where itinerant spacers tried to stretch their terras to buy as much fantasy as their accounts could handle.

"NoT fOr Me," Neeta clarified. "I hAvE a BoNuS fOr YoU. SoOn SoMeOnE wiLL cOmE bY tO hIrE fOr RoBeRt VeNtUra."

The prossy leaned close. "He's bad news. We *all* charge a little extra for going up there. Well, that's the word, anyway. Never been. But we customer service sorts gotta stick together."

"He Is BaD nEwS. We WiLL bE wOrSe NeWs. He TaKeS a DrUg CaLLeD oLyMpUs."

The prossy rolled her eyes. "I know it. Used to be you could take a bit of a break between goes, you know? Now it seems like everyone takes that to get their full value out of an hour. But hey, can't complain, right? Work's work."

"ToNiGhT wiLL bE a LoT oF wOrK. WhEn OnE piLL wEaRs Off MaKe HiM tAkE aNoThEr."

"That's gonna cost. Like a lot."

This was the gambit. By and large, a prossy would charge for just about anything. It was all a matter of settling on a price. But what Neeta was asking was a line few dared cross.

"TwO tHoUsAnD nOw. TeN wHeN vEnTuRa Is DeAd."

The woman mouthed the word, not even daring to say it aloud. "Dead?" She shook her head. "I can't."

"He DeSeRvEs It. So MaNy LiVeS rUiNeD. YoU wiLL bE a HeRo. A rIcH oNe."

She shook her head. "I've never—"

"It WiLL bE eAsY. ThE oNe WhO wiLL cOmE tO hIrE yOu WiLL nOt KnOw. An AgEnT wiLL gEt YoU sAfElY oFF tHe ShIp."

"You'll just have me killed, too."

Neeta shook her head slowly. "I wiLL bE mOrE gRaTeFuL tHaN yOu CaN iMaGiNe."

The prossy narrowed her eyes. "He... hurt you?"

"My MoThEr. I wOuLd Do It MySeLf, BuT..." She looked

the sex worker up and down. "I LaCk ThE... aSSeTs. WiLL yOu Do ThIs?"

A long pause, followed by the heave of exposed cleavage, preceded the answer. "OK. But I want that two big first."

Much as it pained her, Neeta dug into her pocket for a wrapped stack of hardcoin hundreds.

The two parted ways. It would only be a few minutes before Neeta would return as herself to hire Lilac again on behalf of Mort.

━━━

Brassley straddled a ventilation duct, thankful that the flow had been cut to this section of the ship. Too hot. Too cold. Regardless of which setting the ship's life support used, the ducts were never an ideal temperature for the crotch. As she waited just past a cut section at one of the intersections in the network, she listened for signs of the little toy ground-roller Neeta's new friends were employing.

She also played Wiggly Penguins on her datapad because the wait was frankly going to kill her.

Propped on a tangle of pipes beside her was a kiddie-themed duffel intended to carry around spare nappies, both new and used, for the mom on the go. While she *did* have children, and this *was* her nappy duffel, her kiddos were both old enough to operate a washroom and had been for years.

This duffel was filled with lies.

She'd looked at them all as they'd come off the printer. She'd rolled them all up herself. Brassley was less than impressed. Why they'd bribed Tollok 100T for unattended use of the printer and deleting the files afterward was beyond her.

But hey, it was Neeta's plan, and thus far, it was working.

A whiny rumble in the vents alerted Brassley to the

approaching ground-roller. Abandoning her Wiggly Penguins on Island 3.3, she donned her gloves and hunkered low. Brassley liked to think in her blood was the DNA of hunter-gatherers who perched above a stream like this, catching fish with their bare hands in order to survive and carry on the species.

She owed them a good effort for their hard work.

When the rover appeared, Brassley struck. She pinned it down, easily overpowering the toy motor, and used a magnet to clamp the cable to the floor of the vent.

The rover stopped. It reversed, rolled forward, backward, trying to free itself. Brassley opened the knapsack it carried and verified that the paintings inside had been rolled with the picture side inward. Tucking everything back the way she'd found it, she released the magnet, and the roller resumed its trek.

Brassley breathed a sigh.

The wait resumed as the roller's motor faded from hearing.

She wished Neeta had let the rest of them in on the comm channel her patsies were using. It might be nice having a little advance notice. If it was going to be a while, she could use a washroom. It's not like the dopes doing emergency maintenance work needed to come up to this part of the ship. All the main blowers were half a kilometer from here.

After a bladder-threatening wait, the toy ground-roller approached from the opposite direction. With one capture under her belt, Brassley was confident and ready when it came time to wrangle it again.

This time, the payload was worth a fortune. Prograde of two million terras, Neeta promised.

Brassley worked quickly but carefully. She swapped each of the real paintings for the forgeries that had arrived fresh from Tollok's little flatpic pornography shop.

Once the switch was complete, Brassley released the magnet again, and the little laaku-made ground-roller departed, freed of its ineffectual thrashing.

Hefting the duffel, Brassley rushed along the vent, getting ahead of the rumble as she headed for the drop-off point to get the paintings out of her custody.

Because the last thing she needed in her life was getting caught with two million terras worth of stolen art.

Chuck sighed. "We'll probably never know for sure."

Mort rolled his eyes. All for the best. It was a bad idea from the get-go. Why he let himself get dragged into such a cockamamie scheme was beyond him.

No. That wasn't quite true.

Boredom.

Waking hours between amateur terramancy sessions in Mortania had grown especially tedious of late. He'd been taking life as it came, and it just wasn't coming fast enough.

Retreating to the semi-privacy of the room he shared with Brad, Mort found himself a quill and paper.

Becky had relaxed her embargo on magic when Mort had demonstrated he could turn down the arcane deluge that washed away tech like farmsteads behind a burst levee. Operating at a trickle, he could feel like a proper wizard, albeit one exercising extreme self-restraint. Part of that was not having to get up to receive beers from the fridge. Another was not requiring a writing desk to pen a letter.

Flattening a page in front of him, Mort paused a moment to weigh his words carefully.

Azrael, you nitwit.

I said a sabbatical, not a retirement. Haul that bony keester back to the library and start finding me something to do. Otherwise, I swear by Ares's waggling spear, I'll just start hunting down people I don't like and leave it to you to fabricate evidence against them. And you're somewhere down that list.

Now, I realize this missive might meander a bit, but I can't very well leave the wards loose enough for the liaisons to crack them and remake this as tech for long-distance transit. It'll be coming the real old-fashioned way: hand-delivered via starship. I'm giving you to Christmas to get your affairs back in disorder. If not, my New Year's Resolution will be striking a new bargain with your successor.

Mort tried several closings to the letter, recalling the ink from the paper after each, before deciding that if Azrael couldn't deduce who'd sent it, he was useless as a conspirator.

Before sealing the document, however, Mort had one final precaution. He wrote a second letter using the same ink. Were anyone else but the newly anointed Guardian of the Plundered Tomes to gain access to the contents, they'd see only the dummy message.

Much as it shamed him, he'd picked up the idea from Chuck's use of a phony datapad identity.

With a spiteful smirk, he could only *hope* that someone got a look at the message before Azrael took custody.

Dearest Azrael.

*After our last parting, my flower burned for weeks. I can
only imagine you similarly afflicted, for which I believe
one of us owes the other the most abject of apologies. I
would not have contacted you again, except that I felt a
duty to Truth.*

*My belly has swollen past the point of ignoring or
denying any longer. At the advice of my madame, I
intend to bear the child and raise it. The others here at
the home are similarly steadfast in their resolve toward
motherhood. Had any of us known the effects of your
mighty magic on our technological means of preventing
such a personal burden, we might have insisted on other
precautions.*

With Love, Lust & All Else,
Jezebel

Chuckling to himself, Mort folded the letter and sealed it
tight with the best wards old Nebuchadnezzar had taught him.
He'd send it next time they found a planet with a liaison's
office.

———

Neeta strolled the bridge of the *Convoy Queen* as the crew
stood at attention, all lined up for inspection. They weren't the
kind of crew you found on a holovid. These were women and
men who needed a job, had a certain set of skills, and lacked
connections or ambitions, thus ending up out here in the

convoy rather than gainfully employed in the core or even the borderlands.

"Maybe you see for yourself, but you ain't half what was here before," Neeta announced for the group as she walked the line. "Gabbed with all y'all. You lot earned secondsies. Wanna know why? Cuz we're eye-to-eye that my pa was one top-tier asshat. That's it. He weren't nothing to me. Less than.

"My mommy went out an airlock on account of she chose feeding me over paying her whoring fees. Couldn't even take the boot and fly off. No scratch. Didn't even say bye before they flushed her. I was eight. Fucking *eight*. That was near on ten years ago; I'm just makin' it right finally.

"Y'all getting a raise; twice what you made. Ain't no idea how much my old man skimmed. NO IDEA. Wasted it on paint and bank accounts. We gonna fix up this ship, hire better, BE better. With me?"

"Yes, ma'am," came a semi-enthusiastic reply in ragged chorus.

Neeta shrugged. "As ya were. Run the ship. Ain't gonna micro ya."

A pair of bodyguards on loan from Catskill Shulman fell into step behind her as soon as she exited the bridge. It was going to take getting used to, and she wasn't sure whether she wanted protection long-term or not. The general populace believed her father's overdose had been an accident, but a certain Lilac now replanted on Orion IV knew differently, and probably the paramedics, and maybe some of Joe's people.

It gave people ideas.

Neeta tried to force such thoughts from her mind as she entered her quarters.

The bodyguards stationed themselves outside and allowed her to bask in her newfound wealth in private.

These had been Robert Ventura's quarters. While most of

the ship was bare-bones, hard steel, minimum maintenance, this shit was all top-notch. Tile floors, modern electronics, silver fixtures. The furniture had been flushed out the airlock as Neeta's imagination couldn't quit picturing what her father had done all over everything. The bedroom was especially glaring, having replaced the massive, opulent open-faced coffin of a bed with a mattress barely big enough for two.

Neeta entered the washroom and stripped out of her old clothes. She'd pack them away as a reminder but never wear them again.

The shower blasted away grime and layers of dead skin. Lavender shampoo began the slow process of reinvigorating brittle hair. Unaccustomed to the luxury of high-pressure hot water, Neeta allowed herself to melt a little. But as she was relaxing, she couldn't help noticing her own shortcomings.

She stepped out of the shower and looked in the full-wall mirror above the vanity.

Her ribs showed through on both sides of her torso.

The hair might have been a lost cause, better shaved and replaced with a wig until it grew back healthy.

Some of the scars she recalled clearly; others were of mysterious origin.

Her smile was crooked and dingy, but at least she had all her teeth.

Neeta had survived her early life. It was time to do more than survive.

Among the many repairs and upgrades the *Convoy Queen* was going to get was an upgraded medical wing. She wasn't the only permanent resident who could do with better care.

She'd hire a nutritionist for the ship and a personal chef who got paid enough that she'd never worry about poisoned meals. There had to be a dozen vitamins her body was short.

There would be an orthopedist because no teenager should

ache in every joint and an optometrist to add some edges to the general blur of the galaxy.

The ship would get a dentist and a cosmo—maybe several of each, depending on shipwide demand—and she didn't know which would get first crack at her smile.

And once her general health was up to snuff, she'd consider a few upgrades to her curves to make up for what genetics owed her from her mother's side but poor diet had denied her. It had been a wake-up call when that jerk Brad had turned her down. If she couldn't entice a horny teenager, how did she expect to get herself a real man?

Money was the obvious answer.

Neeta didn't want to live her life like that. She wanted love and romance. She wanted ease and luxury. She wanted guys swooning over her and saying to themselves, "And can you believe she's rich, too?" rather than, "Yeah, but she's rich."

As she donned a silk nightgown, she wondered about her cybernetic arm.

She could afford a cloned replacement. Good as new. Better, even; fewer kilometers on it. For three years, she'd gone without. Scrimping and saving, she'd made her way to Phabian, where they never even asked questions, just sat her in a waiting room and grafted on the cybernetic replacement for free, thanks to the Phabian Indigent Support Services. Four years later, it had become part of her.

Out with the old...?

This was Neeta's dream. She had everything her father owed her without having to also survive growing up under his scrutiny. This ship was hers, along with an astonishing array of investments and accounts her lawyers had dug up.

She didn't have to live in squalor.

Neeta could be herself, maybe finally get a chance to discover who that even was.

She didn't need to keep everyone at arm's length anymore.

Staring into the vacant expanse of her new living quarters, it struck her that she didn't need to because everyone was going to be kept at a distance, many by their own choice.

In the kitchen, she found an unopened bottle of Chateau Brioche '23 and popped the cork. She drained the bottle in a long series of gulps and gasps. When she collapsed onto her bed spread-eagle, she resolved to have the mirrored ceiling painted over. The woman staring down at her was a stranger, but one she looked forward to meeting.

The bed was lonely as too much alcohol swirled into her veins. Her body lacked mass to safely distribute so much wine. As sleep rushed in to claim her, Neeta wished for a lover to share this opulence.

It would be different when she was rich and beautiful, lost her shiprat accent, met some fancy people, made fake friends like all the other rich swells.

But just before she passed out, she caught herself wishing Brad Ramsey had stayed behind with her... just for a little while, at least.

****

Ready for more *Black Ocean: Mirth & Mayhem?*
Grab Mission 7, Fly Like an Ego

BOOKS BY J. S. MORIN

Black Ocean

Black Ocean is a vivid 26th century story universe where science and magic coexist—sort of.

Black Ocean: Galaxy Outlaws

Black Ocean: Galaxy Outlaws is a fast-paced fantasy space opera series about the small crew of the *Mobius* trying to squeeze out a living. If you love fantasy and sci-fi, and still lament over the cancellation of *Firefly*, *Black Ocean: Galaxy Outlaws* is the series for you.

Read about the *Black Ocean: Galaxy Outlaws* series and discover where to buy at: galaxyoutlawsmissions.com

Black Ocean: Astral Prime

Co-written with author M.A. Larkin, *Black Ocean: Astral Prime* hearkens back to location-based space sci-fi classics like *Babylon 5* and *Star Trek: Deep Space Nine*. *Astral Prime* builds on the rich *Black Ocean* universe, introducing a colorful cast of characters for new and returning readers alike. Come along for the ride as a minor outpost in the middle of nowhere becomes a key point of interstellar conflict.

Read about the *Black Ocean: Astral Prime* series and discover where to buy at: astralprimemissions.com

Black Ocean: Mercy for Hire

Black Ocean: Mercy for Hire follows the exploits of a pair of do-gooder bounty hunters who care more about saving the day than securing a payday. The series builds on the rich *Black Ocean* universe, centering on a couple of fan-favorites and introducing a colorful cast for new and returning readers alike. Fans of vigilante justice and heroes who exemplify the word will love this series.

Read about *Black Ocean: Mercy for Hire* and discover where to buy at: mercyforhiremissions.com

Black Ocean: Mirth & Mayhem

Black Ocean: Mirth & Mayhem delves into the origins of two vagabonds making their living among the stars. Mort is a wizard coming to grips with a life on the run and estrangement from the comforts and respect he had on Earth. Brad is an impressionable youth, too clever for his—or anyone's—good. And Chuck Ramsey is the mold that Brad's trying to break out of, which is harder than he could ever have dreamed.

Read about *Black Ocean: Mirth & Mayhem* and discover where to buy at: mirthandmayhemmissions.com

Black Ocean: Passage of Time

The year was 2586. A few minutes later, it was 2591. Caught up in a time travel snafu, Eric and Jessie Ramsey become fugitives from the people who want answers as to how they did it—and where their loyalties lie in the galactic war that broke out in their absence.

Read about *Black Ocean: Passage of Time* and discover where to buy at: passageoftimemissions.com

Twinborn Chronicles

The *Twinborn Chronicles* is an epic fantasy saga based on the possibility that our dreams offer us a glimpse into the life of another – another who can get the same glimpse into our world. Read about the *Twinborn Chronicles* and discover where to buy at: twinbornchronicles.com

Twinborn Chronicles: Awakening

Experience the journey of mundane scribe Kyrus Hinterdale who discovers what it means to be Twinborn—and the dangers of getting caught using magic in a world that thinks it exists only in children's stories.

Twinborn Chronicles: War of 3 Worlds

Then continue on into the world of Korr, where the Mad Tinker and his daughter try to save the humans from the oppressive race of Kuduks. When their war spills over into both Tellurak and Veydrus, what alliances will they need to forge to make sure the right side wins?

Project Transhuman

Project Transhuman brings genetic engineering into a post-apocalyptic Earth, 1000 years aliens obliterated all life.

These days, even the humans are built by robots.

Charlie7 is the oldest robot alive. He's seen everything from the fall of mankind at the hands of alien invaders to the rebuilding of a living world from the algae up. But what he hasn't seen in over a thousand years is a healthy, intelligent human. When Eve stumbles into his life, the old robot finally has something worth coming out of retirement for: someone to protect.

Read about all of the *Project Transhuman* books and discover where to buy at: projecttranshuman.com

Sins of Angels

Co-written with author M.A. Larkin, *Sins of Angels* is an epic space opera series set 3000 years after the fall of Earth. With the scope of *Dune* and the adventurous spirit of *Indiana Jones*, it delivers a conflict that spans galaxies and rests on the spirit of brave researcher Professor Rachel Jordan. Follow the complete saga, and watch as the fate of our species hangs in the balance.

Read about *Sins of Angels* and discover where to buy at: sinsofangelsbooks.com

Shadowblood Heir

Shadowblood Heir explores what would happen if the writer of your favorite epic fantasy TV show died before the show ended—and the show was responsible. If you wonder what it would be like if an epic fantasy world invaded our world, this urban fantasy story might give you that glimpse.

Read about *Shadowblood Heir* and discover where to buy at: shadowbloodheir.com

EMAIL INSIDERS

You made it to the end! Maybe you're just persistent, but hopefully that means you enjoyed the book. But this is just the end of one story. If you'd like reading my books, there are always more on the way!

Perks of being an Email Insider include:

- Notification of book releases (often with discounts)
- Inside track on beta reading
- Advance review copies (ARCs)
- Access to Inside Exclusive bonus extras and giveaways
- Best of my blog about fantasy, science fiction, and the art of worldbuilding

Sign up for the my Email Insiders list at: jsmorin.com/updates

ABOUT THE AUTHOR

I am a creator of worlds and a destroyer of words. As a fantasy writer, my works range from traditional epics to futuristic fantasy with starships. I have worked as an unpaid Little League pitcher, a cashier, a student library aide, a factory grunt, a cubicle drone, and an engineer—there is some overlap in the last two.

Through it all, though, I was always a storyteller. Eventually I started writing books based on the stray stories in my head, and people kept telling me to write more of them. Now, that's all I do for a living.

I enjoy strategy, worldbuilding, and the fantasy author's privilege to make up words. I am a gamer, a joker, and a thinker of sideways thoughts. But I don't dance, can't sing, and my best artistic efforts fall short of your average notebook doodle. When you read my books, you are seeing me at my best.

My ultimate goal is to be both clever and right at the same time. I have it on good authority that I have yet to achieve it.

Connect with me online
jsmorin.com

facebook.com/authorjsmorin

twitter.com/authorjsmorin

bookbub.com/authors/j-s-morin

goodreads.com/JSMorin

tiktok.com/@authorjsmorin